From the atomic ashes of the present come the future's menacing wastelands . . .

The Horn of Time chronicles the weird world when civilization is dead, when alien man is a victim of selective killing, mutiny in outer space, extraterrestrial slavery and cosmic war—the millenium when man's most deadly enemy is his inborn human nature!

Also by Poul Anderson

THE DAY OF THEIR RETURN
SATAN'S WORLD
THE HIGH CRUSADE

and published by Corgi Books

THE HORN OF TIME

Poul Anderson

CORGI BOOKS
A DIVISION OF TRANSWORLD PUBLISHERS LTD

THE HORN OF TIME
A CORGI BOOK 0 552 11771 4

First publication in Great Britain

PRINTING HISTORY
Corgi edition published 1981

Corgi Books are published by Transworld Publishers Ltd.,
Century House, 61–63 Uxbridge Road,
Ealing, London, W5 5SA.

Made and printed in the United States of America by
Arcata Graphics, Buffalo, New York.

Contents

To SFWA—
Science Fiction Writers of America—
members, work, and hopes

The Horn of Time the Hunter

Now and then, on that planet, Jong Errifrans thought he heard the distant blowing of a horn. It would begin low, with a pulse that quickened as the notes waxed, until the snarl broke in a brazen scream and sank sobbing away. The first time he started and asked the others if they heard. But the sound was on the bare edge of audibility for him, whose ears were young and sharp, and the men said no. 'Some trick of the wind, off in the cliffs yonder,' Mons Rainart suggested. He shivered. 'The damned wind is always hunting here.' Jong did not mention it again, but when he heard the noise thereafter a jag of cold went through him.

There was no reason for that. Nothing laired in the city but seabirds, whose wings made a white storm over the tower tops and whose flutings mingled with wind skirl and drum roll of surf; nothing more sinister had appeared than a great tiger-striped fish, which patrolled near the outer reefs. And perhaps that was why Jong feared the horn: it gave the emptiness a voice.

At night, rather than set up their glower, the four would gather wood and give themselves the primitive comfort of a fire. Their camping place was in what might once have been a forum. Blocks of polished stone thrust out of the sand and wiry grass that had occupied all streets; toppled colonnades demarked a square. More shelter was offered by the towers clustered in the city's heart, still piercing the sky, the glasit windows still unbroken. But no, those windows were too much like a

7

dead man's eyes, the rooms within were too hushed, now that the machines that had been the city's life lay corroded beneath the dunes. It was better to raise a tent under the stars. Those, at least, were much the same, after twenty thousand years.

The men would eat, and then Regor Lannis, the leader, would lift his communicator bracelet near his mouth and report their day's ransacking. The spaceboat's radio caught the message and relayed it to the *Golden Flyer,* which orbited with the same period as the planet's twenty-one-hour rotation, so that she was always above this island. 'Very little news,' Regor typically said. 'Remnants of tools and so on. We haven't found any bones yet for a radioactivity dating. I don't think we will, either. They probably cremated their dead, to the very end. Mons has estimated that engine block we found began rusting some ten thousand years ago. He's only guessing, though. It wouldn't have lasted at all if the sand hadn't buried it, and we don't know when that happened.'

'But you say the furnishings inside the towers are mostly intact, age-proof alloys and synthetics,' answered Captain Ilmaray's voice. 'Can't you deduce anything from their, well, their arrangement or disarrangement? If the city was plundered—'

'No, sir, the signs are too hard to read. A lot of rooms have obviously been stripped. But we don't know whether that was done in one day or over a period maybe of centuries, as the last colonists mined their homes for stuff they could no longer make. We can only be sure, from the dust, that no one's been inside for longer than I like to think about.'

When Regor had signed off, Jong would usually take out his guitar and chord the songs they sang, the immemorial songs of the Kith, many translated from languages spoken before ever men left Earth. It helped drown out the wind and the surf, booming down on the beach where once a harbor had stood. The fire flared high, picking their faces out of night, tinging plain work clothes with unrestful red, and then guttering down so that shadows swallowed the bodies. They looked much alike, those four men, small, lithe, with sharp, dark features; for the Kith were a folk apart, marrying between their own ships, which carried nearly all traffic among the stars. Since a vessel might be gone from Earth for a century or more, the planetbound civilizations, flaring and dying and reborn like the flames that warmed them now, could not be theirs. The men differed chiefly in age, from the sixty years that furrowed Regor Lannis's skin to the twenty that Jong Errifrans had marked not long ago.

Ship's years, mostly, Jong remembered, and looked up to the Milky Way with a shudder. When you fled at almost the speed of light, time shrank for you, and in his own life he had seen the flower and the fall of an empire. He had not thought much about it then—it was the way of things, that the Kith should be quasi-immortal and the planetarians alien, transitory, not quite real. But a voyage of ten thousand light-years toward galactic center, and back, was more than anyone had ventured before; more than anyone would ever have done, save to expiate the crime of crimes. Did the Kith still exist? Did Earth?

After some days, Regor decided: 'We'd better take a look at the hinterland. We may improve our luck.'

'Nothing in the interior but forest and savannah,' Neri Avelair objected. 'We saw that from above.'

'On foot, though, you see items you miss from a boat,' Regor said. 'The colonists can't have lived exclusively in places like this. They'd need farms, mines, extractor plants, outlying settlements. If we could examine one of those, we might find clearer indications than in this damned huge warren.'

'How much chance would we have, hacking our way through the brush?' Neri argued. 'I say let's investigate some of those other towns we spotted.'

'They're more ruined yet,' Mons Rainart reminded him. 'Largely submerged.' He need not have spoken; how could they forget? Land does not sink fast. The fact that the sea was eating the cities gave some idea of how long they had been abandoned.

9

'Just so.' Regor nodded. 'I don't propose plunging into the woods, either. That'd need more men and more time than we can spare. But there's an outsize beach about a hundred kilometers north of here, fronting on a narrow-mouthed bay, with fertile hills right behind—hills that look as if they ought to contain ores. I'd be surprised if the colonists did not exploit the area.'

Neri's mouth twitched downward. His voice was not quite steady. 'How long do we have to stay on this ghost planet before we admit we'll never know what happened?'

'Not too much longer,' Regor said. 'But we've got to try our best before we do leave.'

He jerked a thumb at the city. Its towers soared above fallen walls and marching dunes into a sky full of birds. The bright yellow sun had bleached out their pastel colors, leaving them bone-white. And yet the view on their far side was beautiful, forest that stretched inland a hundred shades of shadow-rippled green, while in the opposite direction the land sloped down to a sea that glittered like emerald strewn with diamond dust, moving and shouting and hurling itself in foam against the reefs. The first generations here must have been very happy, Jong thought.

'Something destroyed them, and it wasn't simply a war,' Regor said. 'We need to know what. It may not have affected any other world. But maybe it did.'

Maybe Earth lay as empty, Jong thought, not for the first time.

The *Golden Flyer* had paused here to refit before venturing back into man's old domain. Captain Ilmaray had chosen an F9 star arbitrarily, three hundred light-years from Sol's calculated present position. They detected no whisper of the energies used by civilized races, who might have posed a threat. The third planet seemed a paradise, Earth-mass but with its land scattered in islands around a global ocean, warm from pole to pole. Mons Rainart was surprised that the carbon dioxide equilibrium was maintained with so little exposed rock. Then he observed weed mats everywhere on the waters,

10

many of them hundreds of square kilometers in area, and decided that their photosynthesis was active enough to produce a Terrestrial-type atmosphere.

The shock had been to observe from orbit the ruined cities. Not that colonization could not have reached this far, and beyond, during twenty thousand years. But the venture had been terminated; why?

That evening it was Jong's turn to hold a personal conversation with those in the mother ship. He got his parents, via intercom, to tell them how he fared. The heart jumped in his breast when Sorya Rainart's voice joined theirs. 'Oh yes,' the girl said, with an uneven little laugh, 'I'm right here in the apartment. Dropped in for a visit, by chance.'

Her brother chuckled at Jong's back. The young man flushed and wished hotly for privacy. But of course Sorya would have known he'd call tonight. . . . If the Kith still lived, there could be nothing between him and her. You brought your wife home from another ship. It was spaceman's law, exogamy aiding a survival that was precarious at best. If, though, the last Kith ship but theirs drifted dead among the stars; or the few hundred aboard the *Golden Flyer* and the four on this world whose name was lost were the final remnants of the human race—she was bright and gentle and swayed sweetly when she walked.

'I—' He untangled his tongue. 'I'm glad you did. How are you?'

'Lonely and frightened,' she confided. Cosmic interference seethed around her words. The fire spat sparks loudly into the darkness overhead. 'If you don't learn what went wrong here . . . I don't know if I can stand wondering the rest of my life.'

'Cut that!' he said sharply. The rusting of morale had destroyed more than one ship in the past. Although—'No, I'm sorry.' He knew she did not lack courage. The fear was alive in him too that he would be haunted forever by what he had seen here. Death in itself was an old familiar of the Kith. But this time they were returning from a past more ancient than the glaciers and the mammoths had been on Earth when they left. They needed knowledge as much as they needed air, to make sense of the universe. And their first stop in that spiral arm of the Galaxy which had once been home had confronted them with a riddle that looked unanswerable. So deep in history were the roots of the Kith that Jong could recall the symbol of the Sphinx; and suddenly he saw how gruesome it was.

'We'll find out,' he promised Sorya. 'If not here, then when we arrive at Earth.' Inwardly he was unsure. He made small talk and even achieved a joke or two. But afterward, laid out in his sleeping bag, he thought he heard the horn winding in the north.

The expedition rose at dawn, bolted breakfast, and stowed their gear in the spaceboat. It purred from the city on aerodynamic drive, leveled off, flew at low speed not far above ground. The sea tumbled and flashed on the right, the land climbed steeply on the left. No herds of large animals could be seen there. Probably none existed, with such scant room to develop in. But the ocean swarmed. From above Jong could look down into transparent waters, see shadows that were schools of fish numbering in the hundreds of thousands. Further off he observed a herd of grazers, piscine but big as whales, plowing slowly through a weed mat. The colonists must have gotten most of their living from the sea.

Regor set the boat down on a cliff overlooking the bay he had described. The escarpment ringed a curved beach of enormous length and breadth, its sands strewn with rocks and boulders. Kilometers away, the arc closed in on itself, leaving only a strait passage to the ocean. The bay was placid, clear bluish-green beneath the early sun, but not stagnant. The tides of the one big moon must raise and lower it two or three meters in a day, and a river ran in from the southern highlands. Afar Jong could see how shells littered the sand below high-water mark, proof of abundant life. It seemed bitterly unfair to him that the colonists had had to trade so much beauty for darkness.

Regor's lean face turned from one man to the next.

'Equipment check,' he said, and went down the list: ful-gurator, communication bracelet, energy compass, medi-kit—'My God,' said Neri, 'you'd think we were off on a year's trek, and separately at that.'

'We'll disperse, looking for traces,' Regor said, 'and those rocks will often hide us from each other.' He left the rest unspoken: that that which had been the death of the colony might still exist.

They emerged into cool, flowing air with the salt and iodine and clean decay smell of coasts on every Earthlike world, and made their way down the scarp. 'Let's radiate from this point,' Regor said, 'and if nobody has found anything, we'll meet back here in four hours for lunch.'

Jong's path slanted farthest north. He walked briskly at first, enjoying the motion of his muscles, the scrunch of sand and rattle of pebbles beneath his boots, the whistle of the many birds overhead. But presently he must pick his way across drifts of stone and among dark boulders, some as big as houses, which cut him off from the wind and his fellows; and he remembered Sorya's aloneness.

Oh no, not that. Haven't we paid enough? he thought. And, for a moment's defiance: *We didn't do the thing. We condemned the traitors ourselves, and threw them into space, as soon as we learned. Why should we be punished?*

But the Kith had been too long isolated, themselves against the universe, not to hold that the sin and sorrow of one belonged to all. And Tomakan and his coconspira-tors had done what they did unselfishly, to save the ship. In those last vicious years of the Star Empire, when Earthmen made the Kithfolk scapegoats for their wretchedness until every crew fled to await better times, the *Golden Flyer's* captured people would have died hor-ribly—had Tomakan not bought their freedom by betray-ing to the persecutors that asteroid where two other Kith vessels lay, readying to leave the Solar System. How could they afterward meet the eyes of their kindred, in the Council that met at Tau Ceti?

The sentence was just: to go exploring to the fringes of

13

the galactic nucleus. Perhaps they would find the Elder Races that must dwell somewhere; perhaps they would bring back the knowledge and wisdom that could heal man's inborn lunacies. Well, they hadn't; but the voyage was something in itself, sufficient to give the *Golden Flyer* back her honor. No doubt everyone who had sat in Council was now dust. Still, their descendants—

Jong stopped in midstride. His shout went ringing among the rocks.

'What is it? Who called? Anything wrong?' The questions flew from his bracelet like anxious bees.

He stooped over a little heap and touched it with fingers that wouldn't hold steady. 'Worked flints,' he breathed. 'Flakes, broken spearheads . . . shaped wood . . . something—' He scrabbled in the sand. Sunlight struck off a piece of metal, rudely hammered into a dagger. It had been, it must have been fashioned from some of the ageless alloy in the city—long ago, for the blade was worn so thin that it had snapped across. He crouched over the shards and babbled.

And shortly Mons' deep tones cut through: 'Here's another site! An animal skull, could only have been split with a sharp stone, a thong—Wait, wait, I see something carved in this block, maybe a symbol—'

Then suddenly he roared, and made a queer choked gurgle, and his voice came to an end.

Jong leaped erect. The communicator jabbered with calls from Neri and Regor. He ignored them. There was no time for dismay. He tuned his energy compass. Each bracelet emitted a characteristic frequency besides its carrier wave, for location purposes, and—The needle swung about. His free hand unholstered his fulgurator, and he went bounding over the rocks.

As he broke out onto the open stretch of sand the wind hit him full in the face. Momentarily through its shrillness he heard the horn, louder than before, off beyond the cliffs. A part of him remembered fleetingly how one day on a frontier world he had seen a band of huntsmen gallop in pursuit of a wounded animal that wept as it

14

ran, and how the chief had raised a crooked bugle to his lips and blown just such a call.

The note died away. Jong's glance swept the beach. Far down its length he saw several figures emerge from a huddle of boulders. Two of them carried a human shape. He yelled and sprinted to intercept them. The compass dropped from his grasp.

They saw him and paused. When he neared, Jong made out that the form they bore was Mons Rainart's. He swung ghastly limp between his carriers. Blood dripped from his back and over his breast.

Jong's stare went to the six murderers. They were chillingly manlike, half a meter taller than him, magnificently thewed beneath the naked white skin, but altogether hairless, with long webbed feet and fingers, a high dorsal fin, and smaller fins at heels and elbows and on the domed heads. The features were bony, with great sunken eyes and no external ears. A flap of skin drooped from pinched nose to wide mouth. Two carried flint-tipped wooden spears, two had tridents forged from metal—the tines of one were red and wet—and those who bore the body had knives slung at their waists.

'Stop!' Jong shrieked. 'Let him go!'

He plowed to a halt not far off, and menaced them with his gun. The biggest uttered a gruff bark and advanced, trident poised. Jong retreated a step. Whatever they had done, he hated to—

An energy beam winked, followed by its thunderclap. The one who carried Mons' shoulders crumpled, first at the knees, then down into the sand. The blood from the hole burned through him mingled with the spaceman's, equally crimson.

They whirled. Neri Avelair pounded down the beach from the opposite side. His fulgurator spoke again. The shimmering wet sand reflected the blast. It missed, but quartz fused where it struck near the feet of the creatures, and hot droplets spattered them.

The leader waved his trident and shouted. They lumbered toward the water. The one who had Mons' ankles did not let go. The body flapped arms and head as it dragged. Neri shot a third time. Jolted by his own speed, he missed anew. Jong's finger remained frozen on the trigger.

The five giants entered the bay. Its floor shelved rapidly. In a minute they were able to dive below the surface. Neri reached Jong's side and fired, bolt after bolt, till a steam cloud rose into the wind. Tears whipped down his cheeks. 'Why didn't you kill them, you bastard?' he screamed. 'You could have gunned them down where you were!'

'I don't know.' Jong stared at his weapon. It felt oddly heavy.

'They drowned Mons!'

'No . . . he was dead already. I could see. Must have been pierced through the heart. I suppose they ambushed him in those rocks—'

'M-m-maybe. But his body, God damn you, we could'a saved that at least!' Senselessly, Neri put a blast through the finned corpse.

'Stop that,' commanded Regor. He threw himself down, gasping for breath. Dimly, Jong noticed gray streaks in the leader's hair. It seemed a matter of pity and terror that Regor Lannis the unbendable should be whittled away by the tears.

What am I thinking? Mons is killed. Sorya's brother..

Neri holstered his fulgurator, covered his face with both hands, and sobbed.

After a long while Regor shook himself, rose, knelt again to examine the dead swimmer. 'So there were natives here,' he muttered. 'The colonists must not have known. Or maybe they underestimated what savages could do.'

His hands ran over the glabrous hide. 'Still warm,' he said, almost to himself. 'Air-breathing; a true mammal, no doubt, though this male lacks vestigial nipples; real nails on the digits, even if they have grown as thick and sharp as claws.' He peeled back the lips and examined the teeth. 'Omnivore evolving toward carnivore, I'd guess. The molars are still pretty flat, but the rest are bigger than ours, and rather pointed.' He peered into the dimmed eyes. 'Human-type vision, probably less acute. You can't see so far underwater. We'll need extensive study to determine the color-sensitivity curve, if any. Not to mention the other adaptations. I daresay they can stay below for many minutes at a stretch. Doubtless not as long as cetaceans, however. They haven't evolved that far from their land ancestors. You can tell by the fins. Of some use in swimming, but not really an efficient size or shape as yet.'

'You can speculate about that while Mons is being carried away?' Neri choked.

Regor got up and tried in a bemused fashion to brush the sand off his clothes. 'Oh no,' he said. His face worked, and he blinked several times. 'We've got to do something about him, of course.' He looked skyward. The air was full of wings, as the sea birds sensed meat and wheeled insolently close. Their piping overrode the wind. 'Let's get back to the boat. We'll take this carcass along for the scientists.'

Neri cursed at the delay, but took one end of the object. Jong had the other. The weight felt monstrous, and seemed to grow while they stumbled toward the cliffs. Breath rasped in their throats. Their shirts clung to the sweat on them, which they could smell through every sea odor.

Jong looked down at the ugly countenance beneath his hands. In spite of everything, in spite of Mons being dead—oh, never to hear his big laugh again, never to move a chessman or hoist a glass or stand on the thrumming decks with him!—he wondered if a female dwelt somewhere out in the ocean who had thought this face was beautiful.

'We weren't doing them any harm,' said Neri between wheezes.

'You can't . . . blame a poison snake . . . or a carnivore . . . if you come too near,' Jong said.

'But these aren't dumb animals! Look at that braincase. At that knife.' Neri needed a little time before he had the lungful to continue his fury: 'We've dealt with nonhumans often enough. Fought them once in a while.

17

But they had a reason to fight . . . mistaken or not, they did. I never saw or heard of anyone striking down utter strangers at first sight.'

'We may not have been strangers,' Regor said.

'What?' Neri's head twisted around to stare at the older man.

Regor shrugged. 'A human colony was planted here. The natives seem to have wiped it out. I imagine they had reasons then. And the tradition may have survived.'

For ten thousand years or more? Jong thought, shocked. *What horror did our race visit on theirs, that they haven't been able to forget in so many millennia?*.

He tried to picture what might have happened, but found no reality in it, only a dry and somehow thin logic. Presumably this colony was established by a successor civilization to the Star Empire. Presumably that civilization had crumbled in its turn. The settlers had most likely possessed no spaceships of their own; outpost worlds found it easiest to rely on the Kith for what few trade goods they wanted. Often their libraries did not even include the technical data for building a ship, and they lacked the economic surplus necessary to do that research over again.

So—the colony was orphaned. Later, if a period of especially virulent anti-Kithism had occurred here, the traders might have stopped coming; might actually have lost any record of this world's existence. *Or the Kith might have become extinct, but that is not a possibility we will admit*. The planet was left isolated.

Without much land surface it couldn't support a very big population, even if most of the food and industrial resources had been drawn from the sea. However, the people should have been able to maintain a machine culture. No doubt their society would ossify, but static civilizations can last indefinitely.

Unless they are confronted by vigorous barbarians, organized into million-man hordes under the lash of outrage. . . . But was that the answer? Given atomic energy, how could a single city be overrun by any number of neolithic hunters?

18

Attack from within? A simultaneous revolt of every autochthonous slave? Jong looked back to the dead face. The teeth glinted at him. *Maybe I'm softheaded. Maybe these beings simply take a weasel's pleasure in killing.*

They struggled up the scarp and into the boat. Jong was relieved to get the thing hidden in a cold-storage locker. But then came the moment when they called the *Golden Flyer* to report.

'I'll tell his family,' said Captain Ilmaray, most quietly.

But I'll still have to tell Sorya how he looked, Jong thought. The resolution stiffened in him: *We're going to recover the body. Mons is going to have a Kithman's funeral; hands that loved him will start him on his orbit into the sun.*

He had no reason to voice it, even to himself. The oneness of the Kith reached beyond death. Ilmaray asked only if Regor believed there was a chance.

'Yes, provided we start soon,' the leader replied. 'The bottom slopes quickly here, but gets no deeper than about thirty meters. Then it's almost flat to some distance beyond the gate, farther than our sonoprobes reached when we flew over. I doubt the swimmers go so fast they can evade us till they reach a depth too great for a nucleoscope to detect Mons' electronic gear.'

'Good. Don't take risks, though.' Grimly: 'We're too short on future heredity as is.' After a pause, Ilmaray added, 'I'll order a boat with a high-powered magna-screen to the stratosphere, to keep your general area under observation. Luck ride with you.'

'And with every ship of ours,' Regor finished the formula.

As his fingers moved across the pilot board, raising the vessel, he said over his shoulder, 'One of you two get into a spacesuit and be prepared to go down. The other watch the 'scope, and lower him when we find what we're after.'

'I'll go,' said Jong and Neri into each other's mouths. They exchanged a look. Neri's glared.

'Please,' Jong begged. 'Maybe I ought to have shot

them down, when I saw what they'd done to Mons. I don't know. But anyhow, I didn't. So let me bring him back, will you?'

Neri regarded him for nearly a minute more before he nodded.

The boat cruised in slow zigzags out across the bay while Jong climbed into his spacesuit. It would serve as well underwater as in the void. He knotted a line about his waist and adjusted the other end to the little winch by the personnel lock. The metallic strand woven into its plastic would conduct phone messages. He draped a sack over one arm for the, well, the search object, and hoped he would not need the slugthrower at his hip.

'There!'

Jong jerked at Neri's shout. Regor brought the craft to hoverhalt, a couple of meters above the surface and three kilometers from shore. 'You certain?' he asked.

'Absolutely. Not moving, either. I suppose they abandoned him so as to make a faster escape when they saw us coming through the air.'

Jong clamped his helmet shut. External noises ceased. The stillness made him aware of his own breath and pulse and—some inner sound, a stray nerve current or mere imagination—the hunter's horn, remote and triumphant.

The lock opened, filling with sky. Jong walked to the rim and was nearly blinded by the sunlight off the wavelets. Radiance ran to the horizon. He eased himself over the lip. The rope payed out and the surface shut above him. He sank.

A cool green roofed with sunblaze enclosed him. Even through the armor he felt multitudinous vibrations; the sea lived and moved, everywhere around. A pair of fish streaked by, unbelievably graceful. For a heretical instant he wondered if Mons would not rather stay here, lulled to the end of the world.

Cut that! he told himself, and peered downward. Darkness lurked below. He switched on the powerful flash at his belt.

Particles in the water scattered the light, so that he fell

as if through an illuminated cave. More fish passed near. Their scales reflected like jewels. He thought he could make out the bottom now, white sand and uplifted ranges of rock on which clustered many-colored coraloids, growing toward the sun. And the swimmer appeared.

He moved slowly to the fringe of light and poised. In his left hand he bore a trident, perhaps the one which had killed Mons. At first he squinted against the dazzle, then looked steadily at the radiant metal man. As Jong continued to descend he followed, propelling himself with easy gestures of feet and free hand, a motion as lovely as a snake's.

Jong gasped and yanked out his slugthrower.

'What's the matter?' Neri's voice rattled in his earplugs.

He gulped. 'Nothing,' he said, without knowing why. 'Lower away.'

The swimmer came a little closer. His muscles were tense, mouth open as if to bite; but the deep-set eyes remained unwavering. Jong returned the gaze. They went down together.

He's not afraid of me, Jong thought, *or else he's mastered his fear, though he saw on the beach what we can do.*

Impact jarred through his soles. 'I'm here,' he called mechanically. 'Give me some slack and—Oh!'

The blood drained from his head as if an ax had split it. He swayed, supported only by the water. Thunders and winds went through him, and the roar of the horn.

'Jong!' Neri called, infinitely distant. 'Something's wrong, I know it is, gimme an answer, for the love of Kith!'

The swimmer touched bottom too. He stood across from what had belonged to Mons Rainart, the trident upright in his hand.

Jong lifted the gun. 'I can fill you with metal,' he heard himself groan. 'I can cut you to pieces, the way you—you—'

The swimmer shuddered (was the voice conducted to him?) but stayed where he was. Slowly, he raised the

21

trident toward the unseen sun. With a single gesture, he reversed it, thrust it into the sand, let go, and turned his back. A shove of the great legs sent him arrowing off.

The knowledge exploded in Jong. For a century of seconds he stood alone with it.

Regor's words pierced through: 'Get my suit. I'm going after him.'

'I'm all right,' he managed to say. 'I found Mons.'

He gathered what he could. There wasn't much. 'Bring me up,' he said.

When he was lifted from the bay and climbed through the air lock, he felt how heavy was the weight upon him. He let fall the sack and trident and crouched beside them. Water ran off his armor.

The doors closed. The boat climbed. A kilometer high, Regor locked the controls and came aft to join the others. Jong removed his helmet just as Neri opened the sack.

Mons' head rolled out and bounced dreadfully across the deck. Neri strangled a yell.

Regor lurched back. 'They ate him,' he croaked. 'They cut him to pieces for food. Didn't they?'

He gathered his will, strode to the port, and squinted out. 'I saw one of them break the surface, a short while before you came up,' he said between his teeth. Sweat—or was it tears?—coursed down the gullies in his cheeks. 'We can catch him. The boat has a gun turret.'

'No—' Jong tried to rise, but hadn't the strength.

The radio buzzed. Regor ran to the pilot's chair forward, threw himself into it, and slapped the receiver switch. Neri set lips together, picked up the head, and laid it on the sack. 'Mons, Mons, but they'll pay,' he said.

Captain Ilmaray's tones filled the hull: 'We just got word from the observer boat. It isn't on station yet, but the magnascreen's already spotted a horde of swimmers . . . no, several different flocks, huge, must total thousands . . . converging on the island where you are. At the rate they're going, they should arrive in a couple of days.'

Regor shook his head in a stunned fashion. 'How did they know?'

22

'They didn't,' Jong mumbled.

Neri leaped to his feet, a tiger movement. 'That's exactly the chance we want. A couple of bombs dropped in the middle of 'em.'

'You mustn't!' Jong cried. He became able to rise too. The trident was gripped in his hand. 'He gave me this.'

'What?' Regor swiveled around. Neri stiffened where he stood. Silence poured through the boat.

'Down below,' Jong told them. 'He saw me and followed me to the bottom. Realized what I was doing. Gave me this. His weapon.'

'Whatever *for*?'

'A peace offering. What else?'

Neri spat on the deck. 'Peace, with those filthy cannibals?'

Jong squared his shoulders. The armor enclosing him no longer seemed an insupportable burden. 'You wouldn't be a cannibal if you ate a monkey, would you?'

Neri said an obscene word, but Regor suppressed him with a gesture. 'Well, different species,' the pilot admitted coldly. 'By the dictionary you're right. But these killers are sentient. You don't eat another thinking being.'

'It's been done,' Jong said. 'By humans too. More often than not as an act of respect or love, taking some of the person's mana into yourself. Anyway, how could they know what we were? When he saw I'd come to gather our dead, he gave me his weapon. How else could he say he was sorry, and that we're brothers? Maybe he even realized that's literally true, after he'd had a little while to think the matter over. But I don't imagine their traditions are that old. It's enough, it's better, actually, that he confessed we were his kin simply because we also care for our dead.'

'What are you getting at?' Neri snapped.

'Yes, what the destruction's going on down there?' Ilmaray demanded through the radio.

'Wait.' Regor gripped the arms of his chair. His voice fell low. 'You don't mean they're—'

'Yes, I do,' Jong said. 'What else could they be? How could a mammal that big, with hands and brain, evolve

23

on these few islands? How could any natives have wiped out a colony that had atomic arms? I thought about a slave revolt, but that doesn't make sense either. Who'd bother with so many slaves when they had cybernetic machines? No, the swimmers are the colonists. They can't be anything else.'

'Huh?' grunted Neri.

Ilmaray said across hollow space: 'It could be. If I remember rightly, Homo Sapiens is supposed to have developed from the, uh, Neandertaloid type, in something like ten or twenty thousand years. Given a small population, genetic drift, yes, a group might need less time than that to degenerate.'

'Who says they're degenerate?' Jong retorted.

Neri pointed to the staring-eyed head on the deck. 'That does.'

'Was an accident, I tell you, a misunderstanding,' Jong said. 'We had it coming, blundering in blind the way we did. They aren't degenerate, they're just adapted. As the colony got more and more dependent on the sea, and mutations occurred, those who could best take this sort of environment had the most children. A static civilization wouldn't notice what was happening till too late, and wouldn't be able to do anything about it if they did. Because the new people had the freedom of the whole planet. The future was theirs.'

'Yeah, a future of being savages.'

'They couldn't use our kind of civilization. It's wrong for this world. If you're going to spend most of your life in salt water you can't very well keep your electric machines; and flint you can gather almost anywhere is an improvement over metal that has to be mined and smelted.

'Oh, maybe they have lost some intelligence. I doubt that, but if they have, what of it? We never did find the Elder Races. Maybe intelligence really isn't the goal of the universe. I believe, myself, these people are coming back up the ladder in their own way. But that's none of our business.' Jong knelt and closed Mons' eyes. 'We were allowed to atone for our crime,' he said softly. 'The

least we can do is forgive them in our turn. Isn't it? And
. . . we don't know if any other humans are left, anywhere in all the worlds, except us and these. No, we
can't kill them.'

'Then why did they kill Mons?'

'They're air breathers,' Jong said, 'and doubtless they
have to learn swimming, like pinnipeds, instead of having an instinct. So they need breeding grounds. That
beach, yes, that must be where the tribes are headed. A
party of males went in advance to make sure the place
was in order. They saw something strange and terrible
walking on the ground where their children were to be
born, and they had the courage to attack it. I'm sorry,
Mons,' he finished in a whisper.

Neri slumped down on a bench. The silence came
back.

Until Ilmaray said: 'I think you have the answer. We
can't stay here. Return immediately, and we'll get under
weigh.'

Regor nodded and touched the controls. The engine
hummed into life. Jong got up, walked to a port, and
watched the sea, molten silver beneath him, dwindle as
the sky darkened and the stars trod forth.

I wonder what that sound was, he thought vaguely. *A
wind noise, no doubt, as Mons said. But I'll never be
sure.* For a moment it seemed to him that he heard it
again, in the thrum of energy and metal, in the beat of
his own blood, the horn of a hunter pursuing a quarry
that wept as it ran.

A Man to My Wounding

I have slain a man to my wounding, and a young man to my hurt.
—*Genesis*, iv, 23

His names were legion and his face was anybody's. Because a Senator was being hunted, I stood on a corner and waited for him.

The arm gun was a slight, annoying drag under my tunic. Lord knew the thing should be almost a part of me after so many years, but today I had the jaggers. It's always harder on the nerves to defend than to stalk. A vending machine was close by, and I might have bought a reefer, or even a cigaret, to calm me down; but I can't smoke. I got a whiff of chlorine several years ago, during an assassination in Morocco, and the regenerated lung tissue I now use is a bit cranky. Nor did my philosophical tricks work: meditation on the koans of Zen, recital of elementary derivatives and integrals.

I was alone at my post. In some towns, where private autos haven't yet been banned from congested areas, my assignment would have given me trouble. Here, though, only pedestrians and an occasional electroshuttle got between me and my view, kitty-corner across the intersection of Grant and Jefferson to The Sword Called Precious Pearl. I stood as if waiting for a particular ride. A public minivid was on the wall behind me, and after a while I decided it wouldn't hurt to see if anything had happened. Not that I expected it yet. The Senator's escorted plane was still airborne. I hardly thought the enemy would have gotten a bomb aboard. However—

I dropped a coin in the box and turned the dials in search of a newscast.

'. . . development was inevitable, toward greater and greater ferocity. For example, we think of the era between the Peace of Westphalia and the French Revolution as one of limited conflicts. But Heidelberg and Poltava suffice to remind us how easily they got out of hand. Likewise, the relative chivalry of the post-Napoleonic nineteenth century evolved into the trench combat of the First World War, the indiscriminate aerial bombings of the Second, and the atomic horrors of the Third.'

Interested, I leaned closer to the little screen. I only needed one eye to watch that bar. The other could study this speaker. He was a fortyish man with sharp, intelligent features. I liked his delivery, vivid without being sentimental. I couldn't quite place him, though, so I thumbed the info switch. He disappeared for a moment while a sign in the screen told me this was a filmed broadcast of an address by Juan Morales, the new president of the University of California, on the topic: 'Clausewitz's Analysis Reconsidered.'

It was refreshing to hear a college president voice something besides noises about education in the Cybernetic Age. I recalled now that Morales was an historian of note, and moderately active in the Libertarian Party. Doubtless the latter experience had taught him to speak with vigor. The fact that the Enterprise Party had won the last election seemed only to have honed him more fine-edged.

'The Third World War, short and inconclusive as it was, made painfully clear that mass destruction had become ridiculous,' he went on. 'War was traditionally an instrument of national policy, a means of getting acquiescence to something from another state when less drastic measures had failed. But a threat to instigate mutual suicide has no such meaning. At the same time, force remains the *ultima ratio*. It is no use to preach that killing is wrong, that human life is infinitely valuable, and so on. I'm afraid that in point of blunt, regrettable fact, human life has always been a rather cheap commodity. From a man defending his wife against a homicidal maniac, on to the most complex international problems, issues are bound to arise occasionally which cannot be resolved. If these issues are too important to ignore, men will then fight.

'The need of the world today is, therefore, not to plan grandiose renunciations of violence. I know that many distinguished thinkers regard our present system of killing—not whole populations, but the leaders of those populations—as a step forward. Certainly it is more efficient, even more humane, than war. But it does not lead logically to a next step of killing no one at all. Rather, it has merely shifted the means of enforcing the national will.

'Our task is to understand this process. That will not be easy. Assassination evolved slowly, almost unconsciously, like every other viable institution. Like old-fashioned war, it has its own reaction upon the political purposes for which it is used. Also like war, it has its own evolutionary tendencies. Once we thought we had contained war, made it a safely limited duel between gentlemen. We learned better. Let us not make the same complacent mistake about our new system of assassination. Let us—'

'Shine, mister?'

I looked down into a round face and black almond eyes. The boy was perhaps ten years old, small, quick, brilliant in the mandarin tunic affected by most Chinatown youngsters these days. (A kind of defiance, an appeal: Look, we're Americans too, with a special and proud heritage; our ancestors left the old country before the Kung She rose up to make humans into machinery.) He carried a box under his arm.

'What time machine did you get off of?' I asked him.

'A shoe blaster's no good,' he said with a grin. 'I give you a hand shine, just like the Nineties. The Gay Nineties, I mean, not the Nasty Nineties.' As I hesitated: 'You could ride in my cable car, too, only I'm still saving money to get one built. Have a shoe shine and help make San Francisco picturesque again!'

I laughed. 'Sure thing, bucko. I may have to take off in a hurry, though, so let me pay you in advance.'

He made a sparrow's estimate of me. 'Five dollars.'

The cost of a slug of bourbon didn't seem excessive for a good excuse to loiter here. Besides, I like kids. Once I hoped to have a few of my own. Most people in the Bureau of National Protection (good old Anglo-Saxon hypocrisy!) do; they keep regular hours, like any other office workers. However, the field agent—or trigger man, if you don't want euphemisms—has no business getting married. I tried, but shouldn't have. A few years later, when the memory wasn't hurting quite so much, I saw how justified she had been.

I flipped the boy a coin. He speared it in midair and broke out his apparatus. Morales was still talking. The boy cocked an eye at the screen. 'What's he so thermal about, mister? The assassination that's on?'

'The whole system.' I switched the program off hastily, not wanting to draw even this much attention to my real purpose.

But the kid was too bright. Smearing wax on a shoe, he said, 'Gee, I don't get it. How long we been fighting those old Chinese, anyhow? Seven months? And nothing's happened. I bet pretty soon they'll call the whole show off and talk some more. It don't make sense. Why not *do* something first?'

'The two countries might agree on an armistice,' I said with care. 'But that won't be for lack of trying to do each other dirt. A lot of wars in early days got called off too, when neither side found it could make any headway. Do you think it's easy to pot the President, or Chairman Kao-Tsung?'

'I guess not. But Secretive Operative Dan Steelman on the vid—'

'Yeah,' I grunted. 'Him.'

If I'd been one of those granite-jawed microcephalics with beautiful female assistants, whom you see represented as agents of the BNP, everything would have looked clear-cut. The United States of America and the Grand Society of China were in a formally declared state of assassination, weren't they? Our men were gunning for their leaders, and vice versa, right?

Specifically, Senator Greenstein was to address an open meeting in San Francisco tonight, rallying a somewhat reluctant public opinion behind the Administration's firm stand on the Cambodian question. He could do it, too. He was not only floor leader of the Senate Enterprisers, but a brilliant speaker and much admired personally, a major engine of our foreign policy. At any time the Chinese would be happy to bag him. The Washington branch of my corps had already parried several attempts. Here on the West Coast he'd be more vulnerable.

So Secretive Operative Dan Steelman would have arrested the man for whom I stood waiting the minute he walked into the bar where I'd first spotted him. After a fist fight which tore apart the whole saloon, we'd get the secret papers that showed the Chinese consulate was the local HQ of their organization, we'd raid the joint, fade-out to happy ending and long spiel about Jolt, the New Way to Take LSD.

Haw. To settle a single one of those clichés, how stupid is an assassination corps supposed to be? A consulate or embassy is the last place to work out of. Quite apart from its being watched as a matter of routine, diplomatic relations are too valuable to risk by such a breach of international law.

Furthermore, I didn't want to give the Chinese the slightest tip-off that we knew The Sword Called Precious Pearl was a rendezvous of theirs. Johnny Wang had taken months to get himself contacted by their agents, months more to get sucked into their outfit, a couple of years to work up high enough that he could pass on an occasional bit of useful information to us, like the truth about that bar. If they found out that we'd learned this, they'd simply find another spot.

They might also trace back the leak and find Johnny, whom we could ill afford to lose. He was one of our best. In fact, he'd bagged Semyanov by himself, during the Russo-American assassination a decade ago. (He passed as a Buryat Mongol, got a bellhop job in the swank new hotel at Kosygingrad, and smuggled in his equipment piece by piece; when the Soviet Minister of Production finally visited that Siberian town on one of his inspection trips, Johnny Wang was all set to inject the air conditioning of the official suite with hydrogen cyanide.)

My sarcasm surprised the boy. 'Well, gee,' he said, 'I hadn't thought much about it. But I guess it is tough to get a big government man. Real tough. Why do they even try?'

'Oh, they have ways,' I said, not elaborating. The ways can be too unpleasant. Synergic poison, for example. Slip your victim the first component, harmless in itself, weeks ahead of time; then, at your leisure, give him the other dose, mixed in his food or sprayed as an aerosol in his office.

Though nowadays, with the art of guarding a man twenty-four hours a day so highly developed, the trend is back again toward more colorful brute force. If he is not to become a mere figurehead, an important man has to move around, appear publicly, attend conferences; and that sometimes lays him open to his hunters.

'Like what?' the boy persisted.

'Well,' I said, 'if the quarry makes a speech behind a shield of safety plastic, your assassin might wear an artificial arm with a gun inside. He might shoot a thermite slug through the plastic and the speaker, then use a minijato pack to get over the police cordon and across the rooftops.'

Actually, such a method is hopelessly outdated now. And it isn't as horrible as some of the things the laboratories are working on—like remote-control devices to burn out a brain or stop a heart. I went on quickly:

'A state of assassination is similar to a football game, son. A contest, not between individual oafs such as you see on the vid, but between whole organizations. The guy who makes the touchdown depends on line backs, blocking, a long pass. The organizations might probe for months before finding a chink in the enemy armor. But if we knock off enough of their leaders, one after the next, eventually men will come to power who're so scared, or otherwise ready to compromise, that negotiations can recommence to our advantage.'

I didn't add that two can play at that game.

As a matter of fact, we and the Chinese had been quietly nibbling at each other. Their biggest prize so far was the Undersecretary of State; not being anxious to admit failure, our corps let the coroner's verdict of accidental death stand, though we had ample evidence to the contrary. Our best trophy was the Commissar of Internal Waterways for Hopeh Province. That doesn't sound like much till you realize what a lot of traffic still goes by water in China, and that his replacement, correspondingly influential, favored conciliating the Americans.

To date there hadn't been any really big, really decisive coups on either side. But Johnny Wang had learned that four top agents of the Chinese corps were due in town—at the same time as Senator Greenstein.

More than that he had not discovered. The cell type of organization limits the scope of even the most gifted spy. We did not know exactly where, when, or how those agents were to arrive: submarine, false bottom of a truck, stratochute, or what. We did not know their assignments, though the general idea seemed obvious.

Naturally, our outfit was alerted to protect Greenstein and the other bigwigs who were to greet him. Every inch of his route, before and after the speech, had been preplanned in secret and was guarded one way or another. Since the Chinese presumably expected us to be so careful, we were all the more worried that they should slip in their crack hunters at this exact nexus. Why waste personnel on a hopeless task? Or was it hopeless?

Very few men could be spared from guard duty. I was one. They had staked me out in front of The Sword Called Precious Pearl and told me to play by ear.

The shoeshine rag snapped around my feet. The boy's mind had jumped to my example, football, which was a

33

relief. I told him I didn't think we'd make the Rose Bowl this year, but he insisted otherwise. It was a lot of fun arguing with him. I wished I could keep on.

'Well.' He picked up his kit. 'How's that, mister? Pretty good, huh? I gotta go now. If I was you, I wouldn't wait any longer for some old girl.'

His small form vanished in the crowd as I looked at my watch and realized I'd been here almost an hour. What was going on in that building I was supposed to have under surveillance?

What did I already know?

For the thousandth time I ran through the list. We knew the joint was a meeting place of the enemy, that only the owner and a single bartender were Chinese agents, that the rest of the help were innocent and unaware. Bit by bit, we'd studied them and the layout. We'd gotten a girl of our own in, as a waitress. We knew about a storeroom upstairs, always kept locked and burglar-alarmed; we hadn't risked making a sneak entry, but doubtless it was a combination office, file room, and cache for tools and weapons.

Posting myself today at the dragon-shaped bar, I had seen a little man enter. He was altogether ordinary, not to be distinguished from the rest of the Saturday afternoon crowd. His Caucasian face might be real or surgical; the Kung She does have a lot of whites in its pay, just as we have friends of Oriental race. Nothing had differentiated this man except that he spoke softly for a while with that bartender who was a traitor, and then went upstairs. I'd faded back outside. The building had no secret passages or any such nonsense. My man could emerge from the front door onto Grant Street, or out a rear door and a blind alley to Jefferson. My eyes covered both possibilities.

But I'd been waiting an hour now.

He might simply be waiting too. However, the whole thing smelled wrong.

I reached my decision and slipped into the grocery store behind me. A phone booth stood between the bok choy counter and the candied ginger shelf. I dialed local

HQ, slipped a scrambler on the mouthpiece, and told the recorder at the other end what I'd observed and what I planned. There wasn't much the corps could do to help or even to stop me, nailed down as they were by the necessity of protecting the Senator and his colleagues. But if I never reported back, it might be useful for them to know what I'd been about.

I pushed through the crowd, hardly conscious of them. Not that I needed to be. I knew them by heart. The Chinatown citizens, selling their Asian wares, keeping alive their Cantonese language after a century or more over here. Other San Franciscans, looking for amusement. The tourists from Alaska, Massachusetts, Iowa, cratered Los Angeles. The foreigners: Canadians, self-conscious about belonging to the world's wealthiest nation, leaning backward to be good fellows; Europeans, gushing over our old buildings and quaint little shops; Russians, bustling earnestly about with cameras and guidebooks; an Israeli milord, immaculate, reserved, veddy veddy Imperial; a South African or Indonesian in search of a white clerk to order around; and a few Chinese proper—consular officials or commercial representatives—stiff in their drag uniforms but retaining a hint of old Confucian politeness.

Possibly, face remodeled, speech and gait and tastes reconditioned, a Chinese assassin, stalking me. But I couldn't linger to worry about that. I had one of my own to hunt.

Crossing the street, I bent my attention to a koan I'd found helpful before—'What face did you wear before your mother and father conceived you?'—and reentered The Sword Called Precious Pearl in a more relaxed and efficient state. I stood by the entrance a moment, letting my pupils adjust to cool, smoky dimness.

A waitress passed near. Not ours, unfortunately; Joan didn't come on duty till twenty hundred. But I'd read the dossiers on everyone working here. The girl I saw was a petite blonde. Surgery had slanted her blue eyes, which made for a startling effect; the slit-skirt rig she wore on the job added to that. Our inquiries, Joan's reports, everything tagged her as being impulsive, credulous, and rather greedy.

My scheme was chancy, but an instinctive sense of desperation was growing on me. I tapped her arm and donned a sort of smile. 'Excuse me, miss.'

'Yes?' She stopped. 'Can I bring you something, sir?'

'Just a little information. I'm trying to locate a friend.' I slipped her a two-hundred-dollar bill. She nodded very brightly, tucked the bill in her belt pouch, and led me into a cavernous rear booth. I seated myself opposite her and closed the curtains, which I recognized as being of sound-absorbent material.

'Yes, sir?' she invited.

I studied her through the twilight. Muffled, the talk and laughter and footsteps in the barroom seemed far away, not quite real. 'Don't get excited, sis,' I said. 'I'm only looking for a guy. You probably saw him. He came in an hour or so ago, talked to Slim at the bar, then went upstairs. A short baldish fellow. Do you remember?'

Her sudden start took me by surprise. I hadn't expected her to attach any significance to this. 'No,' she whispered. 'I can't—you'd better—'

My pulse flipflopped, but I achieved a chuckle. 'He's a bit shy, but I am too. I just want a chance to talk with him privately, without Slim knowing. It's a business deal, see, and I want him to hear my offer. All I'm asking you to do is tell me if he's still in that storeroom.' As her eyes grew round: 'Yes, I know that's the only possible place for him to have gone. Nothing else up there but an office and such, and those're much too public.'

'I don't know,' she said jaggedly.

'Well, can you find out?' I took my wallet forth, extracted ten kilobuck notes, and shuffled them before her. 'This is yours for the information, and nobody has to be told. In fact, nobody had better be told. Ever.'

Fine beads of sweat glittered on her forehead, catching the wan light. She was scared. Not of me. I don't look tough, and anyhow she was used to petty gangsters. But she had seen something lately that disconcerted her,

36

and when I showed up and touched on the same nerve, it was a shock.

'You under contract here?' I asked, keeping my voice mild.

Her golden head shook.

'Then I'd quit if I were you,' I said. 'Today. Go work somewhere else—the other end of town or a different city altogether.'

I decided to take a further risk, and pulled my right sleeve back far enough for her to glimpse the gun barrel strapped to my forearm.

'This is not a healthy spot,' I went on. 'Slim's got himself mixed up with something.'

I observed her closely. My next line could go flat on its face, it was so straight from the tall corn country. Or it could be a look at hell. She was so rattled by now that I decided she might fall for it.

'Zombie racket,' I said.

'Oh no!' She had shrunk away from me when I showed the gun. At my last words she sagged against the booth wall, and her oblique blue eyes went blank.

I had her hooked. Finding someone who'd believe that story on so little evidence was my first break today. And I needed one for damn sure.

Not that the racket doesn't still exist, here and there. And where it does, it's the ghastliest form of enslavement man has yet invented. But mostly it's been wiped out. Not even legitimate doctors do much psychosurgery any more, and certainly not for zombie merchants. (I refer to the civilized world; totalitarian governments continue to find the procedures useful.)

'You needn't tell Slim, or anyone, why you're quitting,' I said, placing the bills on the table. 'That's jet fare to any other spot in the world, and a stake till you get another job. I understand there are lots of openings around Von Braunsville these days, what with the spaceport being expanded.'

She nodded, stiff in the neck muscles.

'Okay, sis,' I finished. 'Believe me, you needn't get involved in this at all. I just want to know whatever you noticed about that little guy.'

'I saw him talk to Slim and then go upstairs by himself.' She spoke so low I could barely hear. 'That was kind of funny—unusual, I mean. A couple of us girls talked about it. Then I saw him come down again maybe fifteen minutes ago. You know, in this business you got to keep watching everywhere, see if the customers are happy and so on.'

'Uh-huh,' I said. The hope of finding someone this observant was what had brought me back here.

'Well, he came down again,' she said. 'He must have been the same man, because nobody else goes upstairs this time of day. And like you said, he must have gone in the storeroom. They don't ever allow anybody else in there, I guess you know. Well, when he came back, he didn't look like himself. He wore different clothes—red tunic, green pants—and he had thick black hair and walked different, and he carried a little bag or satchel. . . .'

Her voice trailed off. I tried to imagine how a man might strangle himself. Of course that private room would have disguise materials! Not that a skilled agent needs much; it's fantastic what a simple change of posture will do.

My man had altered his looks, collected whatever tools he needed, and sauntered out the front door under my eye like any departing patron.

For a moment I debated coldly whether the enemy knew this place was known to us. Probably not. They had merely been taking a sensible extra precaution. The fault was ours—no, mine—for underestimating their thoroughness.

I looked hard at the girl. Well, I consoled myself, they in their turn had underestimated her and her companions. That's a characteristic failing of the present-day Chinese: to forget that the unregimented common man is able to see and think about things he hasn't been conditioned to see and think about. Nonetheless, they were

38

now ahead on points: because I had no idea where my mouse-turned-cat was bound.

'What's the matter?' The girl's tones became shrill. 'I told you everything I know. It scared me some—wasn't the first funny goings-on I'd noticed here—but I figured it was Slim's business. Then you came along and—Go on! Get out of here!'

'I don't suppose you observed which way he turned as he went out the door?' I asked.

She shook her head The rest of her was shaking too.

I sighed. 'Makes no difference. Well, thanks, sis. If you don't want to attract attention to yourself, you better take a happypill before going back to work.'

She agreed by fumbling in her pouch. So as not to be noticed either, I remained slumped for another few minutes. By then the girl was in orbit. She looked at me rosily, giggled, and said, 'Care to offer me a job yourself? You bought quite a few hours of my time already, you know.'

'I bought your plane fare,' I told her sharply, and left. Sometimes I think a temporary zombie is as gruesome as a permanent one, and more dangerous to civilization.

I had been racing around in my own skull while I waited, like any trapped rat, getting nowhere. A full-dress attempt on Senator Greenstein—even with the hope of also bagging the Governor, the state chairman of the Enterprise Party, and various other jupiters—didn't seem plausible. The only way I could see to get them at once would be by, say, a light super-fast rocket bomber, descending from the stratosphere with ground guidance. But such weapons were banned by the World Disarmament Convention. If the Chinese were about to break *that*. . . . Impossible! What use is it to be the chief corpse in a radioactive desert?

Had the enemy research labs come up with a new technique: the virus gun, the invisibility screen, or any of those dream gadgets? Conceivable, but doubtful. One of our own major triumphs had been a raid on their central R & D plant in Shanghai. We hadn't gotten Grandfather Scientist Feng as hoped, but our agents had machine-gunned a number of valuable lesser men and blown up the main building. There was every reason to believe we were ahead of them in armaments development. The Chinese had nothing we didn't have more of, except perhaps imagination.

And yet they wouldn't slip four of their best killers into this country merely for a lark. The trigger man of real life bears no resemblance to the one on your living-room screen. He has to have the potentialities to start with and such genes are rare. Then a lot of expensive talent goes into training him, peeling off ordinary humanness and installing the needful reflexes. I say this quite without modesty, sometimes wishing to hell I'd flunked out. But at any rate, a top-grade field agent is not expended lightly.

So where was my boy?

I slouched down Grant Street, under the dragon lamps and the peaked tile roofs, thinking that I might already know the answer. The prominent men in this area didn't total so very many. If the agent murdered cleverly enough, as he was trained to do, the result would pass for an accident—though naturally, whenever a big name dies during a state of assassination, the presumption is that it was engineered. The corps can't investigate every case of home electrocution, iodine swallowed by mistake for cough syrup, drowning, suicide. . . . However, no operative kills obscure folk. He has no rational motive for it, and we aren't sadists; we are the kings who die for the people so that little boys with shoeshine kits may not again be fried on molten streets. . . .

I don't know what put the answer in my head. Hunch, subconscious ratiocination, ESP, lucky guess—I just don't know. But I have said that a trigger man is a special and lonely creature. I stood unmoving for an instant. The crowd milled around me, frantic in search of something to fill the rest of the thirty-hour week; I was a million light-years elsewhere, and it was cold.

Then I started running.

I slowed down after a while, which was more efficient under these conditions. I told myself that dsm y

40

equals cos y dy and dcos y equals minus sin y dy, I asked myself how high is green, and presently I arrived in front of New Old St. Mary's church, where the taxis patrol. Somebody's mother was hailing one. As it drew up I pushed her aside, hopped into the bubble, closed it on her gray hairs, and said, 'Berkeley!'

No use urging speed on the pilot. I had to sit and fume. The knowledge that it followed the guide cables faster and more safely than any human chauffeur was scant consolation. I could have browbeaten a man.

The Bay looked silver, down a swooping length of street. The far side was a gleam of towers and delicate colors; they rebuilt well over there, though of course it so happened the bomb had left them a clearer field than in San Francisco. The air was bright and swift, and I could see the giant whale shape of a transpolar merchant submarine standing in past Alcatraz Peace Memorial. Looking at that white spire, I wondered if the old German idea about a human race mind might not be correct; and if so, how grisly a sense of humor does it have?

But I had business on hand. As the taxi swooped into the Bay tunnel I took the city index off its shelf by the phone and leafed through. The address I wanted . . . yes, here . . . 'Twenty-eight seventy-eight Buena Vista,' I told the pilot.

I had no idea if the resident was at home; but neither did my opponent, I supposed. I should call ahead, warn. . . . No. If my antagonist was there already, he mustn't be tipped off that I knew.

We came out onto the freeway and hummed along at an even 150 KPH, another drop in a river of machines. The land climbed rapidly on this side too. We skirted the city within a city which is the UC campus, dropped off the freeway at Euclid, and followed that avenue between canyonlike apartment house walls to Buena Vista. This street was old and narrow and dignified. We had to slow, while I groaned.

'Twenty-eight seventy-eight Buena Vista,' my voice played back to me. The change from my money jingled down. I scooped it up and threw back a coin.

'Drive on past,' I said. 'Let me off around the next bend.'

I heard a clicking. The pilot didn't quite understand, bucked my taped words on to a human dispatcher across the Bay, got its coded orders, and obeyed.

I walked back, the street on my right and a high hedge on my left. Roofs and walls swept away below me, falling to the glitter of great waters. San Francisco and Marin County lifted their somehow unreal hills on the farther side. A fresh wind touched my skin. My footfalls came loudly, and the arm gun weighed a million kilograms.

At the private driveway I turned and walked in. Landscaped grounds enclosed a pleasant modernistic mansion; the University does well by its president. An old gardener was puttering with some roses. I began to realize just how thin my hunch was.

He straightened and peered at me. His face was wizened, his clothes fifty years out of date, his language quaint. 'What's the drag, man?'

'Looking for a chap,' I said. 'Important message. Any strangers been around?'

'Well, I dunno. Like we get a lot of assorted cats.'

I flipped a ten-dollar coin up and down in a cold hand. 'Medium height, thin,' I said. 'Black hair, smallish nose, red tunic, green slacks, carrying a bag.'

'Dunno,' repeated the gardener. 'I mean, like hard to remember.'

'Have a beer on me,' I said, my heartbeat accelerating. I slipped him the coin.

'Cat went in about fifteen minutes ago. Said he was doing the Sonaclean repair bit, like.'

That was a good gimmick. Having your things cleaned with supersonics is expensive, but once you've bought the apparatus it's so damned automatic it diagnoses its own troubles and calls for its own service men. I took the porch steps fast and leaned on the chimes. A voice from the scanner cooed, 'How do you do, sir. Your business, please.'

'I'm from Sonaclean,' I snapped. 'Something appears to be wrong with your set.'

'We have a repairman here now, sir.'

'The continuator doesn't mesh with the hypostat. We got an alarm. You'd better let me talk to him.'

'Very good, sir. One moment, please.'

I waited for about sixty geological epochs till the door was opened manually, by the same house-maintenance technician who'd quizzed me. I'd know that pigeon voice in hell, where as a matter of fact I was.

'This way, please, sir.' She led me down a hall, past a library loaded with books and microspools, and opened a panel on a downward stair. 'Straight that way.'

I looked into fluorescent brightness. Perhaps, I thought in a remote volume of myself, death is not black; perhaps death is just this featureless luminosity, forever. I went down the stairs.

The brains as well as the guts and sinews of the house were down here. A monitor board blinked many red eyes at me; a dust precipitator buzzed within an air shaft. I looked across the glazed plastic floor and saw my man beside an open Sonaclean. His tools were spread out in front of him, and he stood in a posture that looked easy but wasn't. If need be, he could lift his arm and shoot in the same motion that dropped him on the floor and bounced him sideways. And yet his face was kindly, the eyes tired, the skin sagging a bit with surgical middle age.

'Hello,' he said. 'What brings you here?'

He wasn't expecting anyone from the company, of course. He'd disconnected the Sonaclean the moment he arrived. I didn't believe he meant to plant a bomb, or any such elaborate deal. He'd fiddle around awhile, put the machine back together, go upstairs. Maybe this was simply a reconnoitering expedition, or maybe he knew where Morales was and would slay him this same day. Yes, probably the latter.

He'd slip to Juan Morales's study, kill him with a single karate chop, arrange a rug or stool to make the death

43

look accidental, come back to the head of this stairway, and take his leave. Quite likely no one would ever check with the Sonaclean people. Even if somebody did, my man would have vanished long ago; and he was unmemorable. Even here, now, a few meters from him, realizing he must have a gun beneath his tunic sleeve, I found it hard to fix him in my mind. His mediocrity was the work of a great artist.

Was he even the one I sought? His costume combination was being worn this instant by a million harmless citizens; his face was anyone's; the sole deadliness might be housed in my own sick brain.

I grunted. 'Air-filter inspection.'

He turned back to his dojiggling with the machine. And I knew that he was my man.

He took seconds to comprehend what I had said. An American would have protested at once. 'Hey, this is Saturday—' As he whipped about on his heel, my right arm lifted.

Our guns hissed together, but mine was aimed. He lurched back from sheer impact. The needle stood full in his neck. For an instant he sagged against the wall, then blindness seized his eyes. I crouched, waiting for him to lose consciousness.

Instead, the lips peeled from his teeth, his spine arched, and he left the wall in a stiff rigadoon. While he screamed I cursed and ran up the stairs, three at a time.

The housie came into the library from the opposite side. 'What's the matter?' she cried. 'Wait! Wait, you can't—'

I was already at the phone. I fended her off with an elbow while I dialed local HQ, emergency extension. That's one line that is always open, with human monitors, during a state of assassination. I rattled off my identification number and: 'I'm at Twenty-eight seventy-eight Buena Vista, Berkeley. Get a revival squad here. Regular police, if our own medics aren't handy. I plugged one of the opposition with a sleepdart, but they seem to have found some means of sensitizing. He went straight into tetany. . . . Twenty-eight seventy-eight

Buena Vista, yes. Snap to it, and we may still get some use out of him!'

The woman wailed behind me as I pounded back down the stairs. My man was dead, hideously rigid on the floor. I picked him up. A corpse isn't really heavier than an organic, but it feels that way.

'The deep freeze!' I roared. 'Where the obscenity is your freezer? If we can keep the process from—Don't stand there and gawp! Every second at room temperature, more of his brain cells are disintegrating! Do you want them to revive an idiot?'

If he could be resurrected at all. I wasn't sure what had been done to his biochemistry to make him react so to plain old neurocaine. For his sake I could almost hope he wouldn't be viable. I could have done worse in life than be a trigger man, I guess: might have ended on an interrogation team. Not that prisoners undergo torture, nothing that crude, but—Oh, well.

The housie squealed, nearly fainted, but finally led me to a chest behind the kitchen. After which she ran off again. I dumped out several hundred dollars' worth of food to make room for my burden.

As I closed the lid Dr. Juan Morales arrived. He was quite pale, but he asked me steadily, 'What happened to that man?'

'I think he had a heart attack.' I mopped my face and sat down on the coldbox; my knees were like rubber.

Morales stood awhile, regarding me. Some of his color returned, but a bleakness was also gathering in him. 'Miss Thomas said something about your using a needle gun,' he told me, very low.

'Miss Thomas babbles,' I replied.

I saw his fists clench till the knuckles stood white. 'I have a family to think of,' he said. 'Doesn't that give me a right to know the truth?'

I sighed. 'Could be. Come on, let's talk privately. Afterward you can persuade Miss Thomas she misheard me on the phone. Best to keep this off the newscasts, you realize.'

He led me to his study, seated me, and poured some

welcome brandy. Having refilled the glasses and offered cigars, he sat down too. The room was comfortable and masculine, lined with books, a window opening on the bayview grandeur. We smoked in a brief and somehow friendly silence.

At last he said, 'I take it you're from the Bureau of National Protection.'

I nodded. 'Been chasing that fellow. He gave me the slip. I didn't know where he was headed, but I got a hunch that turned out to be correct.'

'But why me?' he breathed—the question that every man must ask at least once in this life.

I chose to interpret it literally. 'They weren't after Senator Greenstein or the other big politicos, not really,' I said. 'They simply picked this time to strike because they knew most of our manpower would be occupied, giving them a clear field everywhere else. I was wrestling with the problem of what they actually planned to do, and a bit from your lecture came back to me.'

'My lecture?' His laugh was nervous, but it meant much that he could laugh in any fashion. 'Which one?'

'On the vid earlier today. About the evolution of war. You were remarking on how it started as a way to break the enemy's will, and finished trying to destroy the enemy himself—not only armies, but factories, fields, cities, women, children. You were speculating if assassination might not develop along similar lines. Evidently it has.'

'But me . . . I am no one! A university president, a minor local figure in a party that lost the last election—'

'It's still a major party,' I said. 'Its turn will come again one of these years. You're among its best thinkers, and young as politicians go. Wilson and Eisenhower were once university presidents too.'

I saw a horror in his eyes, and it was less for himself, who must now live under guard and fear, than for all of us. But that, I suppose, is one of the reasons he was a target.

'Sure,' I said, 'they're gunning for the current President, for Senator Greenstein, for the other Americans who stand in their way in this crisis. Maybe they'll suc-

46

ceed, maybe they won't. In either case, it won't be the last such conflict. They're looking ahead—twenty years, thirty years. As long as we have a state of assassination anyway, they figure they might as well weaken us for the future by killing off our most promising leaders of the next generation.'

I heard a siren. That must be the revival squad. I rose. 'You might try to guess who else they'll hunt,' I told him. 'Three other operatives are loose that I know of, and we may not extract enough information from the one I got.'

He shook his head in a blind, dazed way. 'I'm thinking of more than that,' he said. 'It's like being one of the old atomic scientists on Hiroshima Day. Suddenly an academic proposition has become real.'

I paused at the door. He went on, not looking at me, talking only to his nightmare:

'It's more than the coming necessity of guarding every man who could possibly interest them—though God knows that will be a heavy burden, and when we have to start guarding every gifted child. . . . It's more, even, than our own retaliation in kind; more than the targets spreading from potential leaders to potential scientists to potential teachers and artists and I dare not guess what else. It's that the bounds have been broken.

'I see the rules laid aside once more, in the future. Sneak-attack assassinations. Undeclared assassinations. Assassination with massive weapons that take a thousand bystanders. Permanent states of assassination, dragging on for decade after decade, and no reason for them except the gnawing down of the others because they are the others.

'Whole populations mobilized against the hidden enemy, with each man watching his neighbor like a shark, with privacy, decency, freedom gone. Where is it going to end?' he asked the sky and the broad waters. 'Where is it going to end?'

The High Ones

1

When first he saw the planet, green and blue and cloudy white across many stars, Eben Holbrook had a sense of coming home. He turned from the viewport so that Ekaterina Ivanovna should not see the quick tears in his eyes. The waiting thereafter was long, but his hope upbore him and he stayed free of the quarrels that now flared in the ship. Nerves were worn thin, three parsecs in distance and fifty-eight years in time from Earth; only those who found a way to occupy their hands could endure this final unsureness. Because it might not be final. Tau Ceti might have no world on which men could walk freely. And then it would be back into the night of suspended animation and the night of interstellar space, for no man knew how long.

Holbrook was not a scientist, to examine how safe the planet was for rhesus monkeys and human volunteers. He was a nucleonics engineer. Since his chief, Rakitin, had been killed in the mutiny, he was in charge of the thermonuclear ion-drive. Now that the *Rurik* swung in orbit, he found his time empty, and he was too vauluble for Captain Svenstrup to accept him as a guinea pig on the surface. But he had an idea for improving the engines of the great spaceship's auxiliary boats, and he wrapped himself in a fog of mathematics and made tests and swore and returned to his computations, for all the weeks it took. In spare moments he amused himself with biological textbooks, an old hobby of his.

That was one way to stay out of trouble, and to forget the scorn in certain hazel eyes.

The report came at last: as nearly as could be determined, this world was suitable for men. Safer than Earth, in that no diseases seemed able to attack the newcomers; yet with so similar a biochemistry that many local meats and plants were edible and the seeds and frozen livestock embryos on the ship could surely thrive. Of course, it was always possible that long-range effects existed, or that in some other region than those which had been sampled—

'To hell with that noise,' said Captain Svenstrup. 'We're going down.'

After such news, he would have faced a second mutiny had he decreed otherwise.

They left the *Rurik* in orbit, and the boats gleamed through a high blue heaven—with a tinge of purple, in this somewhat redder sunlight—to land on 'grass,' twinbladed but soft and green, near trees that swayed almost like poplars above a hurried chill river. Not far away lifted steep, darkly forested hills, and beyond them a few snow peaks haunted the sky. That night fires blazed among temporary shelters, folk danced and sang, accordions mingled with banjos, the vodka bottle worked harder than the samovar, and quite likely a few new lives were begun.

There were two moons, one so close that it hurtled between constellations not very different from those of home (what were ten light-years in this god-sized cosmos?) and one stately in a clear crystal dark. The planet's period of rotation was thirty-one hours, its axial tilt 11 degrees; seasons here would not be extreme. They named it New Earth in their various languages, but the Russian majority soon had everyone else calling it Novaya Svoboda, and that quickly became a simple Novaya. Meanwhile, they got busy.

No sign had been found of aborigines to dispute paradise, but one could never be too certain, nor learn too much. Man had had a long time to familiarize himself with Old Earth; the colonists must gain equivalent information in months. So small aircraft were brought down and assembled, and ranged widely.

Holbrook was taking a scout turn, with Ilya Feodorovitch Grushenko and Solomon Levine, when they found the aliens.

They had gone several hundred kilometers from the settlement, to the other side of the mountains. Suddenly the jet flashed over a wooded ridge, and there were the mine pit and the machines and the spaceships.

'Judas priest!' gasped Holbrook. He crammed back the stick. The jet spurted forward.

Grushenko snatched the mike and rattled a report. Only a tape recorder heard him; they had too much work to do in camp. He slammed the mike down and looked grimly at the Americans. 'We had best investigate on foot, comrades,' he said.

'Hadn't we better . . . get home. . . . Maybe they didn't see us go over,' stammered Holbrook.

Grushenko barked a laugh. 'How long do you expect them not to know about us? Let us learn what we can while we can.'

He was a heavy-muscled man, affecting the shaven pate of an Army officer. He made no bones about being an unreconstructed sovietist, he had killed two mutineers before the others overpowered him, and since then his cooperation was surly. But now Levine nodded a bespectacled head and put in: 'He's right, Eben. We can take a walkie-talkie, and the jet's transmitter will relay back to camp.' He lifted a rifle from its rack and sighed. 'I hoped never to carry one of these again.'

'It may not be necessary,' said Holbrook in a desperate voice. 'Those creatures . . . they don't live here . . . they *can't!* Why couldn't we make an, uh, an agreement—'

'Perhaps.' A faraway light flickered in Grushenko's pale eyes. 'Yes, once we learn their language, a treaty

51

might very well be possible, mutual interest and—After all, their level of technology implies they have reached the soviet stage of development.'

"Oh, come off it," said Levine in English.

Holbrook used a downblast to land the jet in a meadow, a few kilometers from the alien diggings. If the craft had not been noticed—and it had gone over high and very quickly—the crew should be able to steal back and observe. . . . He was glad of the imposed silence as they slipped among great shadowy trees; what could he have said, even to Levine? That was how it always went, he thought in a curious irrelevant anguish. He was not much more nervous than the next man, but he had no words at the high moments. His tongue knotted up and he stood like a wooden Indian under the gaze of Ekaterina Ivanovna.

At the end of their walk, they stood peering down a slope through a screen of brush. The land was raw and devastated, must have been worked for centuries. Holbrook remembered an aerial-survey report: curious formations spotted over the whole planet, pits hundreds of meters deep. Yes, those were evidently the remains of similar mines, exhausted and abandoned. How long had the aliens been coming here? The automatons that purred about, digging and carrying, grinding, purifying, loading into the incredibly big and sleek blue spaceships, were such as no one on Earth had ever built.

Levine muttered to a recorder beyond the mountains, 'Looks like lanthanide ores to me. That suggests they've been civilized long enough to use up their home planet's supply, which is one hell of a long time, my friends.' Holbrook thought in a frozenness that it would be very hard to describe the engines down there; they were too foreign, the eye saw them but the mind wasn't yet prepared to register—

'They heard us! They are coming!'

Grushenko's whisper was almost exultant. Holbrook and Levine whirled about. Half a dozen forms were moving at a trot up the slope, directly toward the humans. Holbrook had a lurching impression of creatures dressed in black, with purplish faces muffled by some kind of respirator snout, two legs, two arms, but much too long and thin. He remembered the goblins of his childhood in a lost Maine forest, and a primitive terror took him.

He fought it down while Grushenko stepped out of concealment. 'Friends!' cried the Ukrainian. He raised both hands. 'Friends!' the sun gleamed on his bare head.

An alien raised a tube. Something like a fist struck Holbrook. He went to his knees. A small, hot crater smoked not two meters from him. Grushenko staggered back, his rifle in action. One of the aliens went on its unhuman face. The rest deployed, still running forward. Another explosion outraged the earth; fire crawled up a tree trunk. And another. 'Let's go!' yelled Holbrook.

He saw Levine fall. The little man stared at the cooked remnant of a leg. Holbrook made a grab for him. A gray face turned about. 'No,' said Levine. 'With me you'd never make it.' He cradled his rifle and thumbed it to full automatic. 'No heroics, please. Get the hell back to camp. I'll hold 'em.'

He began to shoot. Grushenko hauled on Holbrook's wrist. Both men pounded down the farther hillside. The snarl of the Terrestrial gun and the boom of the alien blasters followed them. Through the racket, for a second as he ran, Holbrook heard Levine's voice over the walkie-talkie circuit: 'Four of 'em left. More coming out of the spaceships, though. I see three in green clothes. The weapons seem . . . oh, Sarah, help me, the pain . . . packaged energy . . . a super-dielectric, maybe.'

2

The officers of the *Rurik* sat at a long, rough table, under trees whose rustling was not quite like that of any trees on Earth. They looked toward Holbrook and Grushenko, and they listened.

'So we got the jet aloft,' finished Holbrook. 'We, uh, took a long route home—didn't see any, uh, pursuit—

nothing on the radar—' He swore at himself and sat down. 'That's all, I guess.'

Captain Svenstrup stroked his red beard and said heavily: 'Well, ladies and gentlemen. The problem is whether we hide out for a while in hopes of some lucky chance, or evacuate this system at once.'

'You forget that we might fight!'

Ekaterina Ivanovna Saburov said it in a tone that rang. The blood leaped in her wide, high-boned face; under her battered cap, Tau Ceti tinged the short wheaten hair with copper.

'Fight?' Svenstrup skinned his teeth. 'A hundred humans, one spaceship, against a planet?'

The young woman got to her feet. Even through the baggy green tunic and breeches of her uniform—she had clung to it after the mutiny, Red Star and all—she showed big and supple. Holbrook's heart stumbled, rose again, and hurried through an emptiness. She clapped a hand to her pistol and said: 'But they do not belong on this planet. They must be outsiders too, as far from home as we. Shall we run simply because their technology is a little ahead of ours? My nation never felt that was an excuse to surrender her own soil!'

'No,' mumbled Domingo Ximénez. 'Instead you went on to plunder the soil of everyone else.'

'Quiet, there!' said Svenstrup.

His eyes flickered back and forth, down the table and across the camp. Just inside the forest a log cabin stood half built; the Finnish couple who had been erecting it now crouched with the rest of the crew, among guns and silence. The captain tamped tobacco into his pipe and growled: 'We are in this together, Reds and Whites alike. We cannot get up interstellar velocity without filling the ship's reaction-mass tanks, and we would need a week or more to refine so much water, let alone carry out the rest of the drill. Meanwhile, nonhumans are operating a mine and have killed one of us without any provocation we can imagine. They could fly over and drop a nuclear bomb, and that's the end of man on Novaya. I'm astonished that they haven't so far.'

'Or been aware of us, apparently,' murmured Ekaterina. 'They must have arrived later. Did they not notice the *Rurik* in orbit, this camp as they descended? And then our space ferries, our aircraft, have been coming and going. Did they not see our contrails above the mountains? Comrades, this does not make sense.'

Ximénez said, nigh inaudibly: 'How much sense would a mind which is not human make to us?' He crossed himself.

The gesture jarred Holbrook. Had the government of the United World S. S. R. been *that* careless? Crypto-libertarians had gotten aboard the *Rurik*, yes, but a crypto-believer in God?

Grushenko saw the movement too. His mouth lifted sardonically. 'I would expect you to substitute word magic for thought,' he declared. To Svenstrup: 'Captain, somehow we alarmed the aliens. Possibly we happen to resemble another species with which they are at war. They may well be afraid to attack us. Their reasoning processes must be fundamentally akin to ours, simply because the laws of nature are the same throughout the universe. Including those laws of behavior first seen by Karl Marx.'

'Pseudo-laws for a pseudo-religion!' Holbrook was surprised at himself, the way he got it out.

Ekaterina lifted one dark brow and said, 'You do not advance our cause by name-calling, Lieutenant Golbrok.' Dryly: 'Especially when the epithets are not original.'

He retreated into hot-faced wretchedness. *But I love you,* he wanted to call out. *If you are Russian and I am American, if you are Red and I am White, is that a wall between us through all space and time? Can we never be simply human, my tall darling?*

'That will do,' said Svenstrup. 'Let's consider practicalities. Dr. Sugimoto, will you give us the reasons you gave me an hour ago, for assuming that the aliens come from Zolotoy?'

Holbrook started. Zolotoy—the next planet out, gold-colored in the evening sky—the enemy belonged to this

55

same system? Then there was indeed no hope but another plunge into night.

The astronomer rose and said in singsong Russian: 'It is unlikely that anyone would mine the planets of another star on so extensive a scale. It does not appear economically feasible, whether or not one had spaceships which could travel nearly at light-velocity. Now, long-range spectroscopy has shown Zolotoy to have a thin but essentially terrestroid atmosphere. The aliens were not wearing air suits, merely some kind of respirator—I think it reduces the oxygen content of their inhalations—but at any rate, they must use that gas, which is only found free on Zolotoy and Novaya in this system. The high, thin bipedal shape also suggests life evolved for a lower gravity than here. If they actually heard our scouts, such sensitive ears probably developed in more tenuous air.' He sat down again and drummed on the tabletop with jittery fingers.

'I suppose we should have sent boats to every other planet before landing on this one,' said Svenstrup heavily. 'But there was too much impatience, the crew had been locked up too long.'

'The old captain would not have tolerated such indiscipline,' said Ekaterina.

'I won't tolerate much more from you, either.' Svenstrup got his pipe going. 'Here is my plan. We must have more information. I am going to put the *Rurik* into an orbit skewed to the ecliptic plane, as safe a hiding place as any. A few volunteers will stay on Novaya, refining reaction-mass water and maintaining radio contact with the ship. They won't know her orbit; the maser will be controlled by a computer rigged to be blown up in case of trouble. The bulk of our people will wait aboard. One boat will go to Zolotoy and learn whatever may be learned. Its crew will not know the *Rurik's* elements either; they'll report back here. Then we can decide what to do.'

He finished grayly: 'If the boat returns, of course.'

Grushenko stood up. Something like triumph burned in him. 'As a politico-military specialist, I have been selected and trained for linguistic ability,' he said. 'Furthermore, I have had combat experience in suppressing the Brazilian reactionary insurrection. I volunteer for the survey mission.'

'Good,' said Svenstrup. 'We need about two more.'

Ekaterina Ivanovna Saburov smiled and said in her husky voice, 'If a Ukrainian like Comrade Grushenko goes, a Great Russian must also be represented.' Her humor faded and she went on, overriding the captain, 'My sex has nothing to do with it. I am a gunnery officer of the World Soviet Space Fleet. I spent two years on Mars, helping to establish a naval outpost. I feel myself qualified.'

Somehow Holbrook was standing. He stuttered incoherently. Their gaze speared him, a big square-faced young man with rumpled brown hair, nearsighted brown eyes behind contact lenses, body clad in coveralls and boots. He got out at last: 'Let Bunin take my post. I, I, I can find out something about their machinery—'

'Or die with the others,' said Svenstrup. 'We need you in the ship.'

Ekaterina spoke quietly. 'Let him come, Captain. Shall not an American also have the right to dare?'

3

The boat ran swiftly on continuous ion drive until Novaya was only one blue spark of beauty and Zolotoy became an aureate shield. There was much silence aboard. Watching his companions, Holbrook found time to think.

Grushenko said once: 'We are sure to find some point of agreement with them. It is impossible that they could be imperialists.'

Ekaterina curved her lips in a wistful grin. 'Was it not impossible that disloyal personnel could get into the *Rurik*?'

'Traitors on the selection board.' Grushenko's voice darkened. 'They were to choose from many nations; man's first voyage beyond the sun was to be a symbol of

57

the brotherhood of all men in the World Soviets. And who did they pick? Svenstrup! Ximénez! Bunin! Golbrok!'

'No more of that,' said the woman. 'We have one cause now, to survive.'

Grushenko regarded her from narrowed glacial eyes. 'Sometimes I wonder about your own loyalty, Comrade Saburov. You accepted the mutiny as an accomplished fact, without even trying to agitate; you have fully co-operated with Svenstrup's regime; this will not be forgotten when we get back to Earth.'

'Fifty years hence?' she gibed.

'Fifty years is not so long when one has frozen sleep.' Grushenko gave Holbrook a metallic stare. 'True, we have a common interest at the moment. But suppose the aliens can be persuaded to aid one of our factions. Think of that, Comrade Saburov! As for you, *Ami*, consider yourself warned. At the first sign of any double-dealing on your part, I shall kill you.'

Holbrook shrugged. 'I'm not too worried by that kind of threat,' he said. 'You Reds are a minority, you know. And the minority will grow still smaller every year, as people get a taste for liberty.'

'So far there has been nothing the loyal element could do,' said Ekaterina. The frigidity of her tone was a pain within him. But he could not back down, even in words, when men had died in the spaceship's corridors that other men might be free. 'Our time will come. Until then, do not mistake enforced cooperation for willingness. Svenstrup was clever. He spent a year organizing his conspiracy. He called the uprising at a moment when more Whites than Reds were on duty. We others woke up to find him in charge and the weapons borne by his men. What could we do but help man the ship? If anything went wrong with it, no one aboard would ever see daylight again.'

Holbrook fumbled after a reply: 'If the government at home is, uh, so wonderful . . . how did the selection board let would-be rebels like me into the crew? They psych-tested us; they must have known. They must have

58

hoped . . . someday the mutineers . . . or their descendants . . . would come back . . . at the head of a liberating fleet.'

'No!' she cried. Wrath reddened her pale skin. 'Your filthy propaganda has had some results among the crew, yes, but to make everyone an active traitor—the stars will grow cold first!'

Holbrook heard himself speaking fluently; the words sprang out like warriors. 'Why not be honest with yourself? Look at the facts. The expedition was to have spent a total of perhaps fifty years getting to Alpha Centauri, surveying, planting a colony if feasible, and returning to glory. To Earth! Suddenly, because of a handful of rebels, every soul aboard found himself headed for another sun altogether. It would be almost six decades before we got there. Not one of our friends and kin at home would be alive to welcome us back, if we tried to return. But we wouldn't. If Tau Ceti had no suitable planet, we were to go on, maybe for centuries. This generation will never see home again.

'So why did you, why did everyone, not heed the few fanatics like Grushenko, rise up and throw themselves on our guns? Was death too high a price, even the death of the whole ship? Or if so, you still had many years in which to engineer a countermutiny; all of you were awake from time to time, to stand watches. Why didn't you at least conspire?

'You know very well why not! You saw women and grown men crying with joy because they were free. No combination of wakened personnel could give you a majority such as we had. And you noisy Red loyalists have cooperated—under protest, but you have done your assigned duties. Why? Why not set the crew an example? Why haven't you gone on strike? Isn't it because, down inside, not admitting it to yourselves, you also know what a slave pen Earth has become?'

Her hand cracked across his cheek. The blow rang in him. He stood gaping after her, inwardly numbed, as she flung from the control cabin into the passageway beyond.

Grushenko nodded, not without compassion 'They may claim what equality they will. Eben Petrovitch,' he said. It was the first time he had offered that much friendship. 'But they remain women. She will make a good wife for a man who comprehends this is true in her case also.'

'Which I don't?' mumbled Holbrook.

Grushenko shook his head.

And the world Zolotoy grew. They decelerated, backing down upon it. Transistors piloted them; they stared through telescopes and held photographs to the light, hardly believing.

'One city,' whispered Ekaterina. *'One city.'*

Holbrook squinted at the pictures. He was not a military man and had had no experience with aerial shots. However greatly enlarged, they bewildered him. 'A city over the whole planet?' he asked.

Grushenko looked through the viewport. This close, the golden shield was darkly streaked and mottled; here and there lay a quicksilvery gleam. 'Well, about twenty percent of the total area is built over,' he replied. 'But the city forms a unified webwork, like a net spread across the entire oceanless globe. And the open sites are likewise used—plantations, mines, landing fields, transmission stations, I suppose. It is hard to tell, they are so different from any designs we know.'

'No farms?' said Ekaterina. 'Then I imagine their food is synthetic.' Her snub nose wrinkled. 'I should not like that. My folk have been peasants too many centuries.'

'There are no more peasants on Earth,' said Grushenko stiffly. But he shook his hairless skull and clicked his tongue in awe. 'The size of this! The power! How far ahead of us are they? A thousand years? Ten thousand? A million?'

'Not too far ahead to murder poor old Solomon Levine,' said the woman raggedly. Holbrook stole a glance at her. Sweat glistened on the wide, clear brow. So she was afraid too. He felt that the fear knocking under his own ribs would be less if he could have been warding her, but she had been bleak toward him since their quarrel.

60

Well, he thought, *I'm glad she liked Solly. I guess we all did.*

'That was a mistake,' said Grushenko.

'The same mistake could kill us,' said Holbrook.

'It is possible. Are you wishing you had stayed behind?'

The engine growled and grumbled. Fire splashed a darkness burning with stars. At 7800 kilometers out they saw one of the sputniks already identified on photographs. It was colossal, bigger than the *Rurik*, enigmatic with turrets and lights and skeletal towers. It swung past them in a silence like death; the sense of instruments, unliving eyes upon him, prickled in Holbrook's skin.

Down and down. It was not really surprising when the spaceships came. They were larger than the boat, sleekly aerodynamic. Presumably the Zolotoyans did not have to bother about going into orbit and using shuttle rockets; their biggest vessels landed directly. The lean blue shapes maneuvered with precision blasts, so close to absolute efficiency that only the dimmest glow revealed any jets whatsoever.

'Automatic, or remote-controlled,' decided Holbrook in wonder. 'Flesh couldn't take those accelerations.'

Flame blossomed in space, dazzling them so they sat half blind for minutes afterward. 'Magnesium flares,' croaked Grushenko. 'In a perfect circle around us. Exact shooting—to warn us they can put a nuclear shell in our airlock if they wish.' He blinked at the viewport. Zolotoy had subtly changed direction; it was no longer ahead, but below. He chuckled in a parched way. 'We are not about to offer provocation, comrades.'

Muted clanks beat through the hull and their bones. Holbrook saw each torpedo shape as a curve in the ports, like a new horizon. 'Two of them,' said Ekaterina. 'They have laid alongside. With some kind of grapples.' She plucked nervously at the harness of her chair. 'I think they intend to carry us in.'

'We couldn't do that stunt,' muttered Holbrook.

A day came back to him. He had been a country boy, remote even from the collective farms, but once when he was seven years old he sent in a winning Party slogan (he didn't know better then) and was awarded a trip to Europe. Somehow he had entered alone that museum called Notre Dame de Paris; and when he stood in its soaring twilight he realized how helplessly small and young he was.

He cut the engine. For a moment free fall clutched at his stomach, until a renewed pressure swiveled his chair about in the gimbals. The scout boat was being hauled around Zolotoy, but downward as well; they were going to some specific place on the planet for some specific purpose.

He looked through his isolation at Ekaterina, and found her considering him. Angrily, she jerked her face away, reached out, and grasped the hand of Ilya Grushenko.

4

On the way, the humans decompressed their atmosphere until it approximated that of Zolotoy. Sufficient oxygen remained to support lethargic movement, but they donned compressor pumps, capacitor-powered, worn on the back and feeding to a nosepiece. Otherwise they dressed in winter field uniforms and combat helmets. But when Ekaterina fetched her pistol, Grushenko took it from her.

'Would you conquer them with this, Comrade Saburov?' he asked.

She flushed. Her words came muffled through the tenuous air. 'It might give us a chance to break free, if we must escape.'

'They could overhaul this boat in ten seconds. And . . . escape to where? To interstellar space again? I say here we stop, live or die. At best, from here, it will be a weary way to Earth.'

'Forget about Earth,' said Holbrook out of tautness and despair. 'No one is returning to Earth till Novaya is

62

strong enough to stand off a Soviet fleet. Maybe you like to wear the Party's collar. I don't!'

Ekaterina regarded him for a long time. Through the dehumanizing helmet and mask, he still found her beautiful. She replied: 'What kind of freedom is it to become the client state of an almighty Zolotoy? The Soviet overlords are at least human.'

'Watch your language, Comrade Saburov,' snapped Grushenko.

They fell back into silence. Holbrook thought that she had pierced him again. For surely she was right, men could never be free in the shadow of gods. The most benign of super-creatures would breed fear and envy and hatred, by their mere incomprehensible existence; and a society riddled with such disease must soon spew up tyrants. No, better to flee while they had a chance, if they did yet. But how much longer could they endure that devil's voyage?

The linked vessels fell downward on micrometrically calculated blasts. When a landing was finally made, it was so smooth that for a moment Holbrook did not realize he was on Zolotoy.

He unbuckled himself, went to the air-lock controls, and opened the boat. His eardrums popped as pressures equalized; he stepped out into a cold, breezeless air, under a deep violet sky and a shrunken sun. The low gravity, about half Earth's or Novaya's, gave a sense of being in a dream.

Unthinkingly, the three humans moved close together. They stood on square kilometers of glass-slick blackness. A spaceship was descending far off; machines rolled forth to attend it, but otherwise nothing stirred. Yet the emptiness did not suggest decay. Holbrook thought of the bustle around a Terrestrial spaceport. It seemed grubby beside this vast quietude.

The field reached almost to the edge of vision. At one end clustered several towers. They must be two kilometers high, thought Holbrook in the depths of an overwhelmed brain: half a dozen titanic leaps of metal, blended into a harmony that caught at his heart.

'There!'

He turned around. The Zolotoyans were approaching.

They were ten, riding on two small platforms; the propulsive system was not clear, and Holbrook's engineer's mind speculated vaguely about magnetic-field drives. The riders stood, so rigid that not until the flying things had grounded and they had disembarked could the humans be quite sure they were alive.

About them was the same chill beauty as their city bore. Two and a half meters tall they stood, and half the height was lean, narrow-footed legs. Their chests and shoulders were broad, tapering to slender waists; the arms were almost cylindrical but ended in eerily manlike hands. On slim necks poised smooth heads with faces that suggested abstract sculpture—a single slit nostril, delicate lips immobile above a pointed chin, fluted ears, long amber eyes with horizontal pupils. Their skins were a dusky, hairless purple. They were clad identically, in form-fitting black, and carried tubes similar to rifle barrels with bulbous grips, the blast-guns Holbrook remembered.

He thought between thunders: *Why? Why should they ignore us for months, and then attack us so savagely when we dared to look at them, and then fail to pursue us or even search for our camp?*

What are they going to do now?

Grushenko stepped forward. 'Comrades,' he said, raising his palms. His voice came as if from far away; the bare dark spaces ate it down, and Holbrook saw how a suppressed fear made the Ukrainian's visage shiny. But Grushenko pointed at himself. 'Man,' he said. He gestured at the sky. 'From the stars.'

One of the Zolotoyans trilled a few notes. But it was at the others he (?) looked. A gun prodded Holbrook's back.

Ekaterina said with a stiff smile: 'They are not in a conversational mood, Ilya Feodorovitch. Or perhaps only the commissar of interstellar relations is allowed to speak with us.'

Fingers closed on Holbrook's shoulders. He was

pushed along, not violently but with firmness. He mounted one of the platforms. The rest followed him. They rose without sound. Behind them Holbrook saw no one, no thing, on the fused jet of the spacefield, except the machines unloading the other ship and some Zolotoyans casually departing from it. And, yes, the craft that had borne down the Terrestrial boat were being floated off on larger rafts, leaving the boat itself unattended.

'Have they not put a guard on our vessel?' choked Ekaterina.

Grushenko shrugged. 'Why should they? In a civilization this advanced there are no thieves, no vandals, no spies.'

'But—' Holbrook weighed his words. 'See here. If a nonhuman spaceship landed on your front step, wouldn't you at least be curious?'

'They may have a commissar of curiosity,' said Ekaterina. *Her humor shows up at the damnedest times!* thought Holbrook.

Grushenko gave her a hard glance. 'How can you be sure they do not already know everything about us?' he answered.

Ekaterina shook her blonde head. 'Be careful, comrade. At the time we left home, the Academy of Sciences had announced an end to research in telepathy because it was fruitless. By now, probably, such speculations have been classified as a survival of bourgeois subjectivism.'

Did she actually grin as she spoke? Holbrook, unable to share her gallows mirth, lost his question, for now he was flying among the towers, and thence into the city beyond.

No language of Earth had words for what he saw: many-colored pride soaring hundreds of meters skyward, stretching further than his eyes reached. Looped between the clean heights were elevated roadways; he saw pedestrian traffic on them, Zolotoyans in red and blue and green and white as well as black. Uniform and physical appearance seemed to be associated, the reds shorter and more muscular, the greens with outsize heads—but he couldn't be sure, in his few bewildered glimpses. Down below were smaller buildings, domes or more esoteric curves, and a steady flow of noiseless vehicular traffic.

'How many of them?' he breathed.

'Billions, I should think.' Ekaterina laid a hand on his. Her hazel eyes were stretched wide with a sort of terror. 'But everything is so still!'

Great blue-white flashes of energy went between kilometer-high spires. Now and then a musical symbol quivered over the metal reaches of the city. But no one spoke. There was no loitering, no hesitation, no disorder, such as the most sovietized community on Earth would know.

Grushenko's mouth twisted. 'I wonder if we can speak with them,' he admitted in a lost voice. 'What does a dog have to say to a man?' Straightening: 'But we are going to try!'

At the end of a long flight, they landed on a flange, dizzyingly far about the street (?). Watching the Zolotoyan who had the controls, Holbrook found them superbly simple. But at once he was urged through an arched doorway and down a dim corridor of polished blue stone. He saw faint grooves worn in the floor. This place was *old.*

Ekaterina whispered to him, 'Eben Petrovitch'—she had never so called him before—'have you seen a single ornament here? One little picture or calendar or . . . anything? I would give a tooth for something humanly useless.'

'The city is its own ornament,' said Grushenko, louder than required.

They came to a dead-end wall. A black figure touched a stud, and the wall dilated.

Beyond was a room so large that Holbrook could not make out its ceiling through the sourceless muted radiance. But he saw the machine that waited, tier upon tier where tiny red lights crawled like worms, and he saw a hundred silent green-clad Zolotoyans move through the intricate rituals of its operation and servicing. 'A computer,' he mumbled. 'In ten thousand years we may be able to build a computer like that.'

A guard trilled to a technician. The technician waved calmly at some others, who hurried to him. They conferred in a few syllables and turned to the humans with evident purpose.

'*Gospodny pomiluie*,' said Ekaterina. 'It is a . . . a routine! How many star travelers have come here?'

Holbrook was shoved onto a metal plate in the floor. He braced himself for death, for enlightenment, for God. But the machine only blinked and muttered. A technician approached with an instrument, touched it to Holbrook's neck, and withdrew an unfelt few cubic centimeters of blood. He bore it off into the twilight. Holbrook dared not move until commanded.

The machine spoke. Its voice was hard to tell from the sweet Zolotoyan glissandos. The guards leveled their guns. Holbrook gasped and sprang toward Ekaterina. Two black giants caught and held him.

'By heaven,' he howled, foolish and futile in the gloaming, 'if you touch her, you bastards—'

'Wait, Eben Petrovitch,' she called. 'We must submit.'

Fingers moved over his garments. An indicator buzzed. A Zolotoyan reached into Holbrook's pocket and took out a jackknife. His watch was pulled off his wrist, the helmet off his head. 'Judas priest,' he exploded, 'we're being frisked!'

'Potential weapons are being removed,' said Grushenko.

'You mean they don't bother to inspect our spaceboat, but can't tell a watch isn't a deadly weapon—Hey!' Holbrook grabbed at a hand fumbling with his air compressor.

'Don't fight,' said Grushenko. 'We can live without the apparatus.' He began to point at objects, naming them. He was ignored. The prisoners were quickly stripped naked.

5

Beyond the chamber was another hall, and at its end another room. This was a small, bare, windowless cell of the same blue stone. Dull light came from the walls themselves; a waste-disposal hole opened downward; a porous circle in the ceiling gusted fresh air. Otherwise the place was featureless. When the black guards had sent the humans through and the dilated wall had reverted to a barrier, they were alone.

They felt drained and light-headed in the thin atmosphere. Its dryness caught at their throats and its cold gnawed toward their bones. But most terrible, perhaps, was the silence.

Holbrook said at last, for them all: 'Now what?'

Ekaterina's sunlight-colored hair seemed to crackle with frost. Direct desire for her was impossible here, but his awareness of her beauty was redoubled. Suddenly his universe had narrowed to her, with Grushenko hovering on its fringes. Outside lay mystery; the stone walls enclosed him like the curvature of space. She said with a forlorn boldness, the breath smoking from her lips: 'I suppose they will feed us. Otherwise just shooting us would be most logical. But they do not seem to care if we die of pneumonia.'

'Can we eat their food?' replied Holbrook. 'The odds are against it, I'd say. Too many incompatible proteins. The fact we can live on Novaya is nearly a miracle, and Zolotoy isn't that Earthlike.'

'They are not stupid,' snorted Grushenko. 'On the basis of our blood samples they can synthesize an adequate diet for us.'

'And yet they took everything, harmless or not.' Ekaterina sat down, shivering. 'And that computer, did it not give them orders? Is the computer the most powerful brain on this planet?'

'No.' Holbrook joined her on the floor. Oxygen lack slowed his thoughts, but he plowed doggedly toward an idea. 'I don't believe in robots with creative minds. That's what intelligence itself is for. You wouldn't build a machine to eat for you, or . . . or make love . . . or any truly human function. Machines are to help, amplify, supplement. That thing is a gigantic memory bank, a symbolic logic manipulator, what you like; but it is not a personality.'

'But then why did they *obey* it?' she cried.

Grushenko smiled wearily. 'I suppose a clever dog might wonder why a man obeys his slide rule,' he said.

'A good analogy,' Holbrook said. 'Here's my guess. Obviously the Zolotoyans have been civilized for a very long time. So I imagine they visited the nearer stars . . . ages ago, maybe. They took data home with them. That computer is, as Ekaterina said a few hundred years back, the commissar of interstellar relations. It has all the data. It identified us, our home planet—'

'Yes, of course!' exclaimed Grushenko. 'At this moment, the rulers of Zolotoy—whatever they have, perhaps the entire population—they are studying the report on us.'

Ekaterina closed her eyes. 'And what will they decide?' she asked in a dead voice.

'They will send someone to learn our language, or teach us theirs,' said Grushenko. A lift of excitement came to him; he paced back and forth; his feet slapped on the floor and his face became a mask of will. 'Yes. The attack at the mine was a mistake. Our detention now is a precaution. We must assume so, comrades, because if this is not true we are doomed. I suspect that in the past the Zolotoyans encountered another race, a dangerous one, which happens to resemble us. But soon we'll have a chance to reason with them. And they can restore the rightful captaincy of the *Rurik!*'

Holbrook looked up, startled. 'What makes you think they will?'

'We can offer them not so little. It may be necessary to conceal certain matters, in the interests of the larger truth, but—'

'Do you expect to fool a superman?'

'I can try,' said Grushenko simply. 'If there is any need to. Actually, I feel certain they will favor the Red side. Marxist principles would seem to predict as much. However. . . .'

For a minute he rubbed his jaw, pondering. Then he planted himself, big and heavy, in front of Holbrook. He scanned the other man from his height and snapped: 'I will be the only one who talks to them. Do you understand?'

The American stood. The motion made his head swim, but he cocked his fists and said in anger, 'And how do you expect to prevent me . . . comrade?'

'I am the linguist,' said Grushenko. 'I will be talking to them while you are still floundering about trying to tell the phonemes apart. But we are two sovietists here. Between us we can forbid you even to attempt it.'

Holbrook stared at the woman. She rose too, but backed away. One hand lifted to her mouth. 'Ilya Feodorovitch,' she whispered, 'we are three human creatures.'

'Comrade Saburov,' said Grushenko in an iron tone, 'I make this a test of your loyalty. If you wish to commit treason, now is your time.'

Her gaze was wild upon Holbrook. He saw the tides of blood go through her skin, until they ebbed and she stood white and somehow empty.

'Yes, comrade,' she said.

'Good.' Warmth flowed into the deep voice. Grushenko laid his hands upon her shoulders, searched her eyes, abruptly embraced her. 'Thank you, Ekaterina Ivanovna!' He stepped back, and Holbrook saw the thick, hairless countenance blush like a boy's. 'Not for what you do,' breathed Grushenko. 'For what you are.'

She stood quiet a long while. Finally she gave Holbrook a stare gone cat-green and said as if she were a mechanism: 'Your orders are to keep in the background, say nothing, and make no untoward gestures. If need be, we two between us can kill you.'

And she went to a corner and sat down, hugging her knees and burying her face against them.

Holbrook lowered himself. His heart thuttered,

starved for oxygen; he felt the cold strike down his gullet. He had not been so close to weeping since the hour his mother died.

But—

He avoided Grushenko's watchful regard; he retreated into his own mind and buckled on the armor of an engineer's workaday attitude. Here were problems to solve; well, let them be solved, as practical problems in a practical reality. For even this nightmare planet was real. Even it made logical sense. It had to, if only you could see clearly.

He faced a mighty civilization, quite possibly a million years old or more, which maintained interplanetary travel, giant computers, the intricacies of a technology he did not begin to comprehend. But it ignored the unsecret human landings on Novaya. But it attacked senselessly when three strangers appeared—and then did not follow up the attack. But it captured a spacecraft with contemptuous ease, did not bother to look at the booty, shoved the crew through a cut-and-dried routine and into this dungeon.

Cosmos crack open, visitors from another star could not be an everyday affair! And it was understandable the Zolotoyans would remove a prisoner's knife, but why his watch, why his clothes? Well, maybe a watch could be turned into a, oh, a hyperspatial lever. Maybe they knew how to pull some such stunt and dared not assume the newcomers were ignorant of it. But if so, why didn't they take precautions with the outworld boat? Hell, that could be a nuclear time bomb, for all they knew.

The uniforms, the purposefulness, the repulsive degree of discipline, suggested a totalitarian state. Could the Terrestrials only have encountered a few dull-witted subordinates thus far? That would fit the facts. . . . No, it wouldn't, either. Because the overlords, who were not fools, would certainly have been informed, and would have taken immediate steps.

Or would they?

Hobrook gasped. 'God in heaven!'

'What?' Grushenko trod over to him. 'What's wrong?'

71

Holbrook struggled to his feet. 'Look,' he babbled, 'we've got to break out of here. We'll die if we don't. Exposure alone will kill us. And if we don't get back soon, the others will leave this system. I—'

'You will keep silent when the Zolotoyans arrive,' said Grushenko. 'I cannot believe they are planning to liquidate us. But if they are, we can do nothing except take our fate with dignity.'

'But we can, I tell you! We can! Listen—'

The wall dilated.

6

Three guards stood shoulder to shoulder, their guns pointed inward, their lovely unhuman faces blank. A red-clad being, shorter than they, set down a bowl of stew and a container of water. The food was unidentifiable but the odor was savory. Holbrook felt sure it had been manufactured for the captives.

'For the zoo!' he said aloud. And wildly: 'No, for the filing cabinet. File and forget. Lock us up and throw away the key because *there is nothing else they can do with us.*'

Ekaterina caught his arm. 'Back,' she warned.

Grushenko stood making signs and talking, under the amber eyes of the guards. They loomed over him like idols from some unimaginable futurism. And suddenly the hatred seething in Holbrook left him; he knew only pity. He mourned for Zolotoy the damned, which had once been so full of hope.

But he must live. His glance went to Ekaterina. He heard the breath rattle in her nostrils. Already the coryza viruses in her bloodstream were multiplying; chill and oxygen deprivation had weakened her. Fever would come within hours, death within days. And Grushenko would spend days trying to communicate. Or if he could be talked around to Holbrook's beliefs, it might be too late: that electronic idiot savant might decide at any moment that the captives were safest if killed—

'I'm sorry,' said Holbrook. He punched Ekaterina in the stomach.

She lurched and sat down. Holbrook sidestepped the red Zolotoyan, jumped the guards, and seized a blastgun with both hands. He brought up his foot in the same motion, against a bony black-swathed knee, and heaved.

The Zolotoyan staggered. Holbrook reeled back, the gun in his clutch. The other two guards trilled and slewed their own weapons about. Holbrook whipped the blaster to position and squeezed its single switch. Lightning crashed between blue walls.

A signal hooted. Automatic alarm. . . . Guards would come swarming, and their sole reaction would be to kill. 'The computer!' bawled Holbrook. 'We've got to get the computer!' Two hideously charred bodies were collapsing. The stench of burnt flesh grabbed his throat.

'You murdering fool!' Grushenko roared, and leaped at him. Holbrook reversed the blaster and struck with the butt. Grushenko fell to the floor, dazed. The third black Zolotoyan fumbled after a dropped gun. His reactions were as slow as his mates' had been. Holbrook had counted on that; this breed hadn't had any occasion to fight, really fight, for untold generations, and degenerative mutations would have accumulated. Holbrook destroyed him.

'The computer,' he panted. 'It's not a brain, only an automaton.' He reached down, caught Ekaterina by the wrist, and hauled her erect. His heart seemed about to burst; rags of darkness swirled before his eyes. 'But it is the interstellar commissar,' he said. 'The one thing able to decide about us, and now it's sure to decide on killing—'

'You're insane!' shrieked the woman. She clawed after his weapon. He swayed in black mists, batted her away with his own strengthless arms.

'I haven't time now,' he said. 'I love you. Will you come with me?'

He turned and stumbled toward the door, past the scuttering red servitor, over the corpses, and into the hall. The siren squealed before him, around him, through him. His feet were leaden clogs, Christ, what had become of the low gravity— *help me, help me.*

Hands caught his elbow. 'Lean on me, Eben Petrovitch,' she said.

They went down a vaulted corridor full of howling. His temples beat, as if his brain were trying to escape the skull, but vision cleared a little. He saw the wall at the end, stopped by the control stud, and sucked air into his lungs. It burned them, but he felt vigor return.

'Let me go first,' he rasped. 'If the guards get me, remember the computer must be put out of commission. Wait, now.'

The wall gaped for him. He stepped through. The green technicians moved serenely under the huge machine, working as if he did not exist. *In a way,* he thought, *I don't.* He sped across the floor. His footfalls jarred back into his shins. He reached the machine and opened fire.

Thunder roared in the chamber. The technicians twittered and ran around him. One posted himself at a board whose pattern of signaling lights was too intricate for men to grasp, and called out orders. The rest began to fetch replacement parts. And the siren yammered. It was like no alarm on Earth; its voice seemed alive.

Four guards burst in from the outer hall. Holbrook sprang behind a technician, who kept stolidly by his rank of switches. The guards halted, swiveled their heads, and began to cast about like sniffing dogs. Holbrook shot past the green Zolotoyan, dropped one, dropped two. A human would have sacrificed the enemy's living shield to get at the enemy; but no black had ever fired on a green. Another guard approached and was killed. But where had the fourth gotten to?

Holbrook heard the noise and whirled. The gaunt shape had been almost upon him, from the rear. Ekaterina had attacked. They rolled on the floor, she snarling, he with a remote godlike calm even as he wrestled. He got her by the neck. Holbrook clubbed his blaster. After more blows than a man could have survived, the guard slumped.

The woman crawled from beneath, gasping. Hol-

74

brook's strength was fled again, his lungs twin agonies. He sank to the floor beside her. 'Are you all right?' he forced out. 'Are you hurt my dearest?'

'Hold.'

They crouched side by side and turned faces which bled from the nose back toward the machine. Ilya Grushenko stood there. A blaster was poised in his hands. 'Drop your gun or I shoot,' he said. 'You and her both.'

Holbrook's fingers went slack. He heard the remote clatter of his weapon as it struck stone.

'Thank you, Eben Petrovitch,' said Grushenko. 'Now they have proven to them which of our factions is their friend.'

'You don't understand,' Holbrook groaned. 'Listen to me.'

'Be still. Raise your hands. Ah—' Grushenko flicked eyes toward a pair of guards trotting into the room. 'I have them, comrades!' he whooped.

Their fire converged on him. He ceased to be.

Holbrook had already scooped up his own blaster. He shot down the two black Zolotoyans. He rose, swaying and scrabbling after air. Ekaterina huddled at his feet. 'You see,' he said wearily, 'we are in the ultimate collectivist state.' She clung to his knees and wept.

He had not fired many bolts into the computer when its siren went quiet. He assumed that the orders it had been giving were thereby cancelled. He took the woman and they walked away from the pathetically scurrying greens, out into the hallway, past a few guards who ignored them, and so to a flying platform.

7

Under the tall, fair sky of Novaya, Holbrook spoke to the chief of the human outpost. 'You can call them back from the *Rurik*,' he said. 'We're in no more danger.'

'But what are the Zolotoyans?' asked Ximénez. His look went in fear toward the mountains. 'If they are not intelligent beings, then who . . . what . . . created their civilization?'

'Their ancestors,' said Holbrook. 'A very long time ago. They were great once. But they ended with a totalitarian government. A place for everyone and everyone in his place. The holy society, whose very stasis was holy. Specialized breeds for the different jobs. Some crude attempts at it have been made on Earth. Egypt didn't change for thousands of years after the pyramids had been built. Diocletian, the Roman emperor, made every occupation hereditary. The Hindus had their caste system. China, Korea, Japan tried to cut themselves off from the outside world, from any challenge or alteration. And isn't communism supposed, by definition, to be perfect, so that new ideas must be heretical? I doubt if many more starships will come from Earth, unless and until the Soviets are overthrown.

'The Zolotoyans were unlucky. Their attempt succeeded.'

He shrugged. 'When one individual is made exactly like another—when independent thought is no longer needed, is actually forbidden—what do you expect?' he said. 'Evolution gets rid of organs which have stopped being useful. That includes the thinking brain.'

'But what you saw—space travel, police functions, chemical analysis and synthesis, maintaining those wonderful machines—it is all done by instinct?' protested Ximénez. 'No, I cannot believe it.'

'Instinct isn't completely rigid, you know,' Holbrook said. 'Even a simple one-loop homeostatic circuit is amazingly flexible and adaptive. Think of ants or bees or termites on Earth. In their own ways, they have societies as intricate as anything known to us. They actually have a sort of stylized language, as do our neighbors here. In fact, I suspect the average ant faces more variety and more problems in his life than the average Zolotoyan. Remember, they have no natural enemies anymore; and for tens of thousands of years, every job on that highly automated planet has been stereotyped.

'The mine guards on Novaya paid no attention to our

rocket trails beyond the mountains because—oh, to their perception it couldn't have been very different from lightning, say. But they had long ago evolved an instinct to shoot at unknown visitors, simply because large Novayan animals could interfere with operations. At home, they have no occasion to fight. But apparently the guards, like the green technicians, have an inborn obedience to computer signals.'

'Yes,' said Ximénez. 'That computer, what was it?'

Holbrook sighed. 'I suppose it was built in the last dying age of reason. Some atavistic genius (how lonely he must have been!) realized what was happening to his people. Sooner or later, visitors from space were sure to arrive. He wanted to give his descendants at least a little defense against them. He built that machine, which could try to identify them, could give a few simple orders about their disarmament and care and feeding, that sort of thing. Maybe he used some controlled mutation process to breed the technicians that serviced it, and the obedience of the guards. Or maybe he only needed to institute a set of regulations. There'd be natural selection toward an instinct. . . . It really wasn't much he could do. A poor, clumsy protection against diseases we might have carried, or wanton looting, or. . . .'

Holbrook looked upward. Wind caressed him. Sunlight fell between summer leaves like a benediction on him and the young woman who held his hand. Now, when the technical problem was disposed of, he spoke more slowly and awkwardly:

'I could pity the Zolotoyans, except that they're beyond it. They are as empty of selfhood as ants. But the one who built the computer, can't you almost hear him back in time, asking for our mercy?'

Ximénez nodded. 'Well,' he said, 'I do not see why we should not let the . . . fauna . . . live. We can learn a great deal from them.'

'Including this,' said Holbrook: 'that it shall not happen to our race. We've a planet here, and a whole new science to master. Our children or our grandchildren will return to Earth, undefeatable.'

Ekaterina's grasp released his, but her arm went about his waist, drawing him close as if he were a shield. Her eyes ranged the great strange horizon and she asked, very low, 'After all those years away, do you think they will care about Earth?'

'I don't know,' said Holbrook. He tasted the light like rain on his uplifted face. 'I don't know, dearest, really. I don't even know if it matters.'

The Man Who Came Early

Yes, when a man grows old he has heard so much that is strange there's little more can surprise him. They say the king in Miklagard has a beast of gold before his high seat which stands up and roars. I have it from Eilif Eiriksson, who served in the guard down yonder, and he is a steady fellow when not drunk. He has also seen the Greek fire used, it burns on water.

So, priest, I am not unwilling to believe what you say about the White Christ. I have been in England and France myself, and seen how the folk prosper. He must be a very powerful god, to ward so many realms . . . and did you say that everyone who is baptized will be given a white robe? I would like to have one. They mildew, of course, in this cursed wet Iceland weather, but a small sacrifice to the house-elves should—No sacrifices? Come now! I'll give up horseflesh if I must, my teeth not being what they were, but every sensible man knows how much trouble the elves make if they're not fed.

Well, let's have another cup and talk about it. How do you like the beer? It's my own brew, you know. The cups I got in England, many years back. I was a young man then . . . time goes, time goes. Afterward I came back and inherited this my father's farm, and have not left it since. Well enough to go in viking as a youth, but grown older you see where the real wealth lies: here, in the land and the cattle.

Stoke up the fires, Hjalti. It's getting cold. Sometimes

I think the winters are colder than when I was a boy. Thorbrand of the Salmondale says so, but he believes the gods are angry because so many are turning from them. You'll have trouble winning Thorbrand over, priest. A stubborn man. Myself I am open-minded, and willing to listen at least.

Now, then. There is one point on which I must set you right. The end of the world is not coming in two years. This I know.

And if you ask me how I know, that's a very long tale, and in some ways a terrible one. Glad I am to be old, and safe in the earth before that great tomorrow comes. It will be an eldritch time before the frost giants fare loose . . . oh, very well, before the angel blows his battle horn. One reason I hearken to your preaching is that I know the White Christ will conquer Thor. I know Iceland is going to be Christian erelong, and it seems best to range myself on the winning side.

No, I've had no visions. This is a happening of five years ago, which my own household and neighbors can swear to. They mostly did not believe what the stranger told; I do, more or less, if only because I don't think a liar could wreak so much harm. I loved my daughter, priest, and after the trouble was over I made a good marriage for her. She did not naysay it, but now she sits out on the ness-farm with her husband and never a word to me; and I hear he is ill pleased with her silence and moodiness, and spends his nights with an Irish leman. For this I cannot blame him, but it grieves me.

Well, I've drunk enough to tell the whole truth now, and whether you believe it or not makes no odds to me. Here . . . you, girls! . . . fill these cups again, for I'll have a dry throat before I finish the telling.

It begins, then, on a day in early summer, five years ago. At that time, my wife Ragnhild and I had only two unwed children still living with us: our youngest son Helgi, of seventeen winters, and our daughter Thorgunna, of eighteen. The girl, being fair, had already had suitors. But she refused them, and I am not one who would compel his daughter. As for Helgi, he was ever a lively one, good with his hands but a breakneck youth. He is now serving in the guard of King Olaf of Norway. Besides these, of course, we had about ten housefolk—two thralls, two girls to help with the women's work, and half a dozen hired carles. This is not a small stead.

You have seen how my land lies. About two miles to the west is the bay; the thorps at Reykjavik are some five miles south. The land rises toward the Long Jökull, so that my acres are hilly; but it's good hay land, and we often find driftwood on the beach. I've built a shed down there for it, as well as a boathouse.

We had had a storm the night before—a wild huge storm with lightning flashes across heaven, such as you seldom get in Iceland—so Helgi and I were going down to look for drift. You, coming from Norway, do not know how precious wood is to us here, who have only a few scrubby trees and must get our timber from abroad. Back there men have often been burned in their houses by their foes, but we count that the worst of deeds, though it's not unheard of.

As I was on good terms with my neighbors, we took only hand weapons. I bore my ax, Helgi a sword, and the two carles we had with us bore spears. It was a day washed clean by the night's fury, and the sun fell bright on long, wet grass. I saw my stead lying rich around its courtyard, sleek cows and sheep, smoke rising from the roofhole of the hall, and knew I'd not done so ill in my lifetime. My son Helgi's hair fluttered in the low west wind as we left the buildings behind a ridge and neared the water. Strange how well I remember all which happened that day; somehow it was a sharper day than most.

When we came down to the strand, the sea was beating heavy, white and gray out to the world's edge, smelling of salt and kelp. A few gulls mewed above us, frightened off a cod washed onto the shore. I saw a litter of no few sticks, even a baulk of timber . . . from some ship carrying it that broke up during the night, I suppose. That was a useful find, though as a careful man I would later sacrifice to be sure the owner's ghost wouldn't plague me.

We had fallen to and were dragging the baulk toward the shed when Helgi cried out. I ran for my ax as I looked the way he pointed. We had no feuds then, but there are always outlaws.

This newcomer seemed harmless, though. Indeed, as he stumbled nearer across the black sand I thought him quite unarmed and wondered what had happened. He was a big man and strangely clad—he wore coat and breeches and shoes like anyone else, but they were of odd cut, and he bound his trousers with leggings rather than straps. Nor had I ever seen a helmet like his: it was almost square, and came down to ward his neck, but it had no nose guard. And this you may not believe, but it was not metal yet had been cast in one piece!

He broke into a staggering run as he drew close, flapped his arms and croaked something. The tongue was none I had heard, and I have heard many; it was like dogs barking. I saw that he was clean-shaven and his black hair cropped short, and thought he might be French. Otherwise he was a young man, and good-looking, with blue eyes and regular features. From his skin I judged that he spent much time indoors. However, he had a fine manly build.

'Could he have been shipwrecked?' asked Helgi.

'His clothes are dry and unstained,' I said; 'nor has he been wandering long, for no stubble is on his chin. Yet I've heard of no strangers guesting hereabouts.'

We lowered our weapons, and he came up to us and stood gasping. I saw that his coat and the shirt underneath were fastened with bonelike buttons rather than laces, and were of heavy weave. About his neck he had fastened a strip of cloth tucked into his coat. These garments were all in brownish hues. His shoes were of a sort new to me, very well stitched. Here and there on his coat were bits of brass, and he had three broken stripes on each sleeve; also a black band with white letters, the same letters being on his helmet. Those were not runes, but Roman—thus: MP. He wore a broad belt, with a small clublike thing of metal in a sheath at the hip and also a real club.

'I think he must be a warlock,' muttered my carle Sigurd. 'Why else so many tokens?'

'They may only be ornament, or to ward against witchcraft,' I soothed him. Then, to the stranger: 'I hight Ospak Ulfsson of Hillstead. What is your errand?'

He stood with his chest heaving and a wildness in his eyes. He must have run a long way. At last he moaned and sat down and covered his face.

'If he's sick, best we get him to the house,' said Helgi. I heard eagerness; we see few new faces here.

'No . . . no . . .' The stranger looked up. 'Let me rest a moment—'

He spoke the Norse tongue readily enough, though with a thick accent not easy to follow and with many foreign words I did not understand.

The other carle, Grim, hefted his spear. 'Have vikings landed?' he asked.

'When did vikings ever come to Iceland?' I snorted. 'It's the other way around.'

The newcomer shook his head as if it had been struck. He got shakily to his feet. 'What happened?' he said. 'What became of the town?'

'What town?' I asked reasonably.

'Reykjavik!' he cried. 'Where is it?'

'Five miles south, the way you came—unless you mean the bay itself,' I said.

'No! There was only a beach, and a few wretched huts, and—'

'Best not let Hjalmar Broadnose hear you call his thorp that,' I counseled.

'But there was a town!' he gasped. 'I was crossing the street in a storm, and heard a crash, and then I stood on the beach and the town was gone!'

'He's mad,' said Sigurd, backing away. 'Be careful. If

83

he starts to foam at the mouth, it means he's going berserk.'

'Who are you?' babbled the stranger. 'What are you doing in those clothes? Why the spears?'

'Somehow,' said Helgi, 'he does not sound crazed, only frightened and bewildered. Something evil has beset him.'

'I'm not staying near a man under a curse!' yelped Sigurd, and started to run away.

'Come back!' I bawled. 'Stand where you are or I'll cleave your louse-bitten head.'

That stopped him, for he had no kin who would avenge him; but he would not come closer. Meanwhile the stranger had calmed down to the point where he could talk somewhat evenly.

'Was it the *aitsjbom*?' he asked. 'Has the war started?'

He used that word often, *aitsjbom*, so I know it now, though unsure of what it means. It seems to be a kind of Greek fire. As for the war, I knew not which war he meant, and told him so.

'We had a great thunderstorm last night,' I added. 'And you say you were out in one too. Maybe Thor's hammer knocked you from your place to here.'

'But where is here?' he answered. His voice was more dulled than otherwise, now that the first terror had lifted.

'I told you. This is Hillstead, which is on Iceland.'

'But that's where I was!' he said. 'Reykjavik . . . what happened? Did the *aitsjbom* destroy everything while I lay witless?'

'Nothing has been destroyed,' I said.

'Does he mean the fire at Olafsvik last month?' wondered Helgi.

'No, no, no!' Again he buried his face in his hands. After a while he looked up and said: 'See here. I am *Sardjant* Gerald Robbins of the United States Army base on Iceland. I was in Reykjavik and got struck by lightning or something. Suddenly I was standing on the beach, and lost my head and ran. That's all. Now, can you tell me how to get back to the base?'

84

Those were more or less his words, priest. Of course, we did not grasp half of them, and made him repeat several times and explain. Even then we did not understand, save that he was from some country called the United States of America, which he said lies beyond Greenland to the west, and that he and some others were on Iceland to help our folk against their foes. This I did not consider a lie—more a mistake or imagining. Grim would have cut him down for thinking us stupid enough to swallow that tale, but I could see that he meant it.

Talking cooled him further. 'Look here,' he said, in too calm a tone for a feverish man, 'maybe we can get at the truth from your side. Has there been no war you know of? Nothing which—Well, look here. My country's men first came to Iceland to guard it against the Germans. Now it is the Russians, but then it was the Germans. When was that?'

Helgi shook his head. 'That never happened that I know of,' he said. 'Who are these Russians?' We found out later that the Gardariki folk were meant. 'Unless,' Helgi said, 'the old warlocks—'

'He means the Irish monks,' I explained. 'A few dwelt here when the Norsemen came, but they were driven out. That was, hm, somewhat over a hundred years ago. Did your kingdom once help the monks?'

'I never heard of them!' he said. The breath sobbed in his throat. 'You . . . didn't you Icelanders come from Norway?'

'Yes, about a hundred years ago,' I answered patiently. 'After King Harald Fairhair laid the Norse lands under him and—'

'A *hundred years ago!*' he whispered. I saw whiteness creep up beneath his skin. 'What year is this?'

We gaped at him. 'Well, it's the second year after the great salmon catch,' I tried.

'What year after Christ, I mean,' he prayed hoarsely.

'Oh, so you are a Christian? Hm, let me think. . . . I talked with a bishop in England once, we were holding him for ransom, and he said . . . let me see . . . I think he said this Christ man lived a thousand years ago, or maybe a little less.'

'A thousand—' Something went out of him. He stood with glassy eyes—yes, I have seen glass, I told you I am a traveled man—he stood thus, and when we led him toward the garth he went like a small child.

You can see for yourself, priest, that my wife Ragnhild is still good to look upon even in eld, and Thorgunna took after her. She was—is tall and slim, with a dragon's hoard of golden hair. She being a maiden then, the locks flowed loose over her shoulders. She had great blue eyes and a heart-shaped face and very red lips. Withal she was a merry one, and kindhearted, so that she was widely loved. Sverri Snorrason went in viking when she refused him, and was slain, but no one had the wit to see that she was unlucky.

We led this Gerald Samsson—when I asked, he said his father was named Sam—we led him home, leaving Sigurd and Grim to finish gathering the driftwood. Some folks would not have a Christian in their house, for fear of witchcraft, but I am a broad-minded man, and Helgi, at his age, was wild for anything new. Our guest stumbled over the fields as if blind, but seemed to rouse when we entered the yard. His gaze went around the buildings that enclosed it, from the stables and sheds to the smokehouse, the brewery, the kitchen, the bathhouse, the god shrine, and thence to the hall. And Thorgunna was standing in the doorway.

Their gazes locked for a little, and I saw her color but thought nothing of it then. Our shoes rang on the flagging as we crossed the yard and kicked the dogs aside. My two thralls halted in cleaning the stables to gawp, until I got them back to work with the remark that a man good for naught else was always a pleasing sacrifice. That's one useful practice you Christians lack; I've never made a human offering myself, but you know not how helpful is the fact that I could do so.

We entered the hall, and I told the folk Gerald's name and how we found him. Ragnhild set her maids hopping, to

86

stoke up the fire in the middle trench and fetch beer, while I led Gerald to the high seat and sat down by him. Thorgunna brought us the filled horns. His standing was not like yours, for whom we use our outland cups.

Gerald tasted the brew and made a face. I felt somewhat offended, for my beer is reckoned good, and asked him if aught was wrong. He laughed with a harsh note and said no, but he was used to beer that foamed and was not sour.

'And where might they make such?' I wondered testily.

'Everywhere,' he said. 'Iceland, too—no. . . .' He stared before him in an empty wise. 'Let's say . . . in Vinland.'

'Where is Vinland?' I asked.

'The country to the west whence I came. I thought you knew. . . . Wait a bit.' He frowned. 'Maybe I can find out something. Have you heard of Leif Eiriksson?'

'No,' I said. Since then it has struck me that this was one proof of his tale, for Leif Eiriksson is now a well-known chief; and I also take more seriously those yarns of land seen by Bjarni Herjulfsson.

'His father, Eirik the Red?' went on Gerald.

'Oh yes,' I said. 'If you mean the Norseman who came hither because of a manslaughter, and left Iceland in turn for the same reason, and has now settled with his friends in Greenland.'

'Then this is . . . a little before Leif's voyage,' he muttered. 'The late tenth century.'

'See here,' broke in Helgi, 'we've been forbearing with you, but now is no time for riddles. We save those for feasts and drinking bouts. Can you not say plainly whence you come and how you got here?'

Gerald looked down at the floor, shaking.

'Let the man alone, Helgi,' said Thorgunna. 'Can you not see he's troubled?'

He raised his head and gave her the look of a hurt dog that someone has patted. The hall was dim; enough light seeped in the loft windows that no candles were lit, but not enough to see well by. Nevertheless, I marked a reddening in both their faces.

Gerald drew a long breath and fumbled about. His clothes were made with pockets. He brought out a small parchment box and from it took a little white stick that he put in his mouth. Then he took out another box, and a wooden stick therefrom which burst into flame when scratched. With the fire he kindled the stick in his mouth, and sucked in the smoke.

We stared. 'Is that a Christian rite?' asked Helgi.

'No . . . not just so.' A wry, disappointed smile twisted his lips. 'I thought you'd be more surprised, even terrified.'

'It's something new,' I admitted, 'but we're a sober folk on Iceland. Those fire sticks could be useful. Did you come to trade in them?'

'Hardly.' He sighed. The smoke he breathed in seemed to steady him, which was odd, because the smoke in the hall had made him cough and water at the eyes. 'The truth is, well, something you will not believe. I can hardly believe it myself.'

We waited. Thorgunna stood leaning forward, her lips parted.

'That lightning bolt—' Gerald nodded wearily. 'I was out in the storm, and somehow the lightning must have smitten me in just the right way, a way that happens only once in many thousands of times. It threw me back into the past.'

Those were his words, priest. I did not understand, and told him so.

'It's hard to grasp,' he agreed. 'God give that I'm merely dreaming. But if this is a dream I must endure till I awaken. . . . Well, look. I was born one thousand, nine hundred and thirty-three years after Christ, in a land to the west which you have not yet found. In the twenty-fourth year of my life, I was in Iceland with my country's war host. The lightning struck me, and now, now it is less than one thousand years after Christ, and yet I am here—almost a thousand years before I was born, I am here!'

We sat very still. I signed myself with the Hammer

88

and took a long pull from my horn. One of the maids whimpered, and Ragnhild whispered so fiercely I could hear: 'Be still. The poor fellow's out of his head. There's no harm in him.'

I thought she was right, unless maybe in the last part. The gods can speak through a madman, and the gods are not always to be trusted. Or he could turn berserker, or he could be under a heavy curse that would also touch us.

He slumped, gazing before him. I caught a few fleas and cracked them while I pondered. Gerald noticed and asked with some horror if we had many fleas here.

'Why, of course,' said Thorgunna. 'Have you none?'

'No.' He smiled crookedly. 'Not yet.'

'Ah,' she sighed, 'then you *must* be sick.'

She was a level-headed girl. I saw her thought, and so did Ragnhild and Helgi. Clearly, a man so sick that he had no fleas could be expected to rave. We might still fret about whether we could catch the illness, but I deemed this unlikely; his woe was in the head, maybe from a blow he had taken. In any case, the matter was come down to earth now, something we could deal with.

I being a godi, a chief who holds sacrifices, it behooved me not to run a stranger out. Moreover, if he could fetch in many of those fire-kindling sticks, a profitable trade might be built up. So I said Gerald should go to rest. He protested, but we manhandled him into the shut-bed, and there he lay tired and was soon asleep. Thorgunna said she would take care of him.

The next eventide I meant to sacrifice a horse, both because of the timber we had found and to take away any curse that might be on Gerald. Furthermore, the beast I picked was old and useless, and we were short of fresh meat. Gerald had spent the morning lounging moodily around the garth, but when I came in at noon to eat I found him and my daughter laughing.

'You seem to be on the road to health,' I said.

'Oh yes. It . . . could be worse for me.' He sat down

at my side as the carles set up the trestle table and the maids brought in the food. 'I was ever much taken with the age of the vikings, and I have some skills.'

'Well,' I said, 'if you have no home, we can keep you here for a while.'

'I can work,' he said eagerly. 'I'll be worth my pay.'

Now I knew he was from afar, because what chief would work on any land but his own, and for hire at that? Yet he had the easy manner of the high-born, and had clearly eaten well throughout his life. I overlooked that he had made me no gifts; after all, he was shipwrecked.

'Maybe you can get passage back to your United States,' said Helgi. 'We could hire a ship. I'm fain to see that realm.'

'No,' said Gerald bleakly. 'There is no such place. Not yet.'

'So you still hold to that idea you came from tomorrow?' grunted Sigurd. 'Crazy notion. Pass the pork.'

'I do,' said Gerald. Calm had come upon him. 'And I can prove it.'

'I don't see how you speak our tongue, if you hail from so far away,' I said. I would not call a man a liar to his face, unless we were swapping friendly brags, but—

'They speak otherwise in my land and time,' he said, 'but it happens that in Iceland the tongue changed little since the old days, and because my work had me often talking with the folk, I learned it when I came here.'

'If you are a Christian,' I said, 'you must bear with us while we sacrifice tonight.'

'I've naught against that,' he said. 'I fear I never was a very good Christian. I'd like to watch. How is it done?'

I told him how I would smite the horse with a hammer before the god, and cut its throat, and sprinkle the blood about with willow twigs; thereafter we would butcher the carcass and feast. He said hastily:

'Here's my chance to prove what I am. I have a weapon that will kill the horse with, with a flash of lightning.'

'What is it?' I wondered. We crowded around while he

took the metal club out of its sheath and showed it to us. I had my doubts; it looked well enough for hitting a man, I reckoned, but had no edge, though a wondrously skillful smith had forged it. 'Well, we can try,' I said. You have seen how on Iceland we are less concerned to follow the rites exactly than they are in the older countries.

Gerald showed us what else he had in his pockets. There were some coins of remarkable roundness and sharpness, though neither gold nor true silver; a tiny key; a stick with lead in it for writing; a flat purse holding many bits of marked paper. When he told us gravely that some of this paper was money, Thorgunna herself had to laugh. Best was a knife whose blade folded into the handle. When he saw me admiring that, he gave it to me, which was well done for a shipwrecked man. I said I would give him clothes and a good ax, as well as lodging for as long as needful.

No, I don't have the knife now. You shall hear why. It's a pity, for that was a good knife, though rather small.

'What were you ere the war arrow went out in your land?' asked Helgi. 'A merchant?'

'No,' said Gerald. 'I was an . . . *endjinur* . . . that is, I was learning how to be one. A man who builds things, bridges and roads and tools . . . more than just an artisan. So I think my knowledge could be of great value here.' I saw a fever in his eyes. 'Yes, give me time and I'll be a king.'

'We have no king on Iceland,' I grunted. 'Our forefathers came hither to get away from kings. Now we meet at the Things to try suits and pass new laws, but each man must get his own redress as best he can.'

'But suppose the one in the wrong won't yield?' he asked.

'Then there can be a fine feud,' said Helgi, and went on to relate some of the killings in past years. Gerald looked unhappy and fingered his *gun*. That is what he called his firespitting club. He tried to rally himself with a joke about now, at last, being free to call it a gun instead of something else. That disquieted me, smacked of witchcraft, so to change the talk I told Helgi to stop his

91

chattering of manslaughter as if it were sport. With law shall the land be built.

'Your clothing is rich,' said Thorgunna softly. 'Your folk must own broad acres at home.'

'No,' he said, 'our . . . our king gives each man in the host clothes like these. As for my family, we owned no farm, we rented our home in a building where many other families also dwelt.'

I am not purse-proud, but it seemed me he had not been honest, a landless man sharing my high seat like a chief. Thorgunna covered my huffiness by saying, 'You will gain a farm later.'

After sunset we went out to the shrine. The carles had built a fire before it, and as I opened the door the wooden Odin appeared to leap forth. My house has long invoked him above the others. Gerald muttered to my daughter that it was a clumsy bit of carving, and since my father had made it I was still more angry with him. Some folk have no understanding of the fine arts.

Nevertheless, I let him help me lead the horse forth to the altar stone. I took the blood bowl in my hands and said he could now slay the beast if he would. He drew his gun, put the end behind the horse's ear, and squeezed. We heard a crack, and the beast jerked and dropped with a hole blown through its skull, wasting the brains. A clumsy weapon. I caught a whiff, sharp and bitter like that around a volcano. We all jumped, one of the women screamed, and Gerald looked happy. I gathered my wits and finished the rest of the sacrifice as was right. Gerald did not like having blood sprinkled over him, but then he was a Christian. Nor would he take more than a little of the soup and flesh.

Afterward Helgi questioned him about the gun, and he said it could kill a man at bowshot distance but had no witchcraft in it, only use of some tricks we did not know. Having heard of the Greek fire, I believed him. A gun could be useful in a fight, as indeed I was to learn, but it did not seem very practical—iron costing what it does, and months of forging needed for each one.

I fretted more about the man himself.

And the next morning I found him telling Thorgunna a great deal of foolishness about his home—buildings as tall as mountains, and wagons that flew, or went without horses. He said there were eight or nine thousand thousands of folk in his town, a burgh called New Jorvik or the like. I enjoy a good brag as well as the next man, but this was too much, and I told him gruffly to come along and help me get in some strayed cattle.

After a day scrambling around the hills I saw that Gerald could hardly tell a cow's bow from her stern. We almost had the strays once, but he ran stupidly across their path and turned them, so the whole work was to do again. I asked him with strained courtesy if he could milk, shear, wield scythe or flail, and he said no, he had never lived on a farm.

'That's a shame,' I remarked, 'for everyone on Iceland does, unless he be outlawed.'

He flushed at my tone. 'I can do enough else,' he answered. 'Give me some tools and I'll show you good metalwork.'

That brightened me, for truth to tell, none of our household was a gifted smith. 'That's an honorable trade,' I said, 'and you can be of great help. I have a broken sword and several bent spearheads to be mended, and it were no bad idea to shoe the horses.' His admission that he did not know how to put on a shoe was not very dampening to me then.

We had returned home as we talked, and Thorgunna came angrily forward. 'That's no way to treat a guest, Father,' she said. 'Making him work like a carle, indeed!'

Gerald smiled. 'I'll be glad to work,' he said. 'I need a . . . a stake . . . something to start me afresh. Also, I want to repay a little of your kindness.'

Those words made me mild toward him, and I said it was not his fault they had different ways in the United States. On the morrow he could begin in the smithy, and I would pay him, yet he would be treated as an equal since craftsmen are valued. This earned him black looks from the housefolk.

That evening he entertained us well with stories of his home; true or not, they made good listening. However, he had no real polish, being unable to compose a line of verse. They must be a raw and backward lot in the United States. He said his task in the war host had been to keep order among the troops. Helgi said this was unheard of, and he must be bold who durst offend so many men, but Gerald said folk obeyed him out of fear of the king. When he added that the term of a levy in the United States was two years, and that men could be called to war even in harvest time, I said he was well out of a country with so ruthless and powerful a lord.

'No,' he answered wistfully, 'we are a free folk, who say what we please.'

'But it seems you may not do as you please,' said Helgi.

'Well,' Gerald said, 'we may not murder a man just because he aggrieves us.'

'Not even if he has slain your own kin?' asked Helgi.

'No. It is for the . . . the king to take vengeance, on behalf of the whole folk whose peace has been broken.'

I chuckled. 'Your yarns are cunningly wrought,' I said, 'but there you've hit a snag. How could the king so much as keep count of the slaughters, let alone avenge them? Why, he'd not have time to beget an heir!'

Gerald could say no more for the laughter that followed.

The next day he went to the smithy, with a thrall to pump the bellows for him. I was gone that day and night, down to Reykjavik to dicker with Hjalmar Broadnose about some sheep. I invited him back for an overnight stay, and we rode into my steading with his son Ketill, a red-haired sulky youth of twenty winters who had been refused by Thorgunna.

I found Gerald sitting gloomily on a bench in the hall. He wore the clothes I had given him, his own having been spoilt by ash and sparks; what had he awaited, the fool? He talked in a low voice with my daughter.

94

'Well,' I said as I trod in, 'how went the tasks?'

My man Grim snickered. 'He ruined two spearheads, but we put out the fire he started ere the whole smithy burned.'

'How's this?' I cried. 'You said you were a smith.'

Gerald stood up, defiant. 'I worked with different tools, and better ones, at home,' he replied. 'You do it otherwise here.'

They told me he had built up the fire too hot; his hammer had struck everywhere but the place it should; he had wrecked the temper of the steel through not knowing when to quench it. Smithcraft takes years to learn, of course, but he might have owned to being not so much as an apprentice.

'Well,' I snapped, 'what can you do, then, to earn your bread?' It irked me to be made a ninny of before Hjalmar and Ketill, whom I had told about the stranger.

'Odin alone knows,' said Grim. 'I took him with me to ride after your goats, and never have I seen a worse horseman. I asked him if maybe he could spin or weave, and he said no.'

'That was no question to ask a man!' flared Thorgunna. 'He should have slain you for it.'

'He should indeed,' laughed Grim. 'But let me carry on the tale. I thought we would also repair your bridge over the foss. Well, he *can* barely handle a saw, but he nigh took his own foot off with the adze.'

'We don't use those tools, I tell you!' Gerald doubled his fists and looked close to tears.

I motioned my guests to sit down. 'I don't suppose you can butcher or smoke a hog, either,' I said, 'or salt a fish or turf a roof.'

'No.' I could hardly hear him.

'Well, then, man, whatever can you do?'

'I—' He could get no words out.

'You were a warrior,' said Thorgunna.

'Yes, that I was!' he said, his face kindling.

'Small use on Iceland when you have no other skills,' I grumbled, 'but maybe, if you can get passage to the eastlands, some king will take you in his guard.' Myself I doubted it, for a guardsman needs manners that will do credit to his lord; but I had not the heart to say so.

Ketill Hjalmarsson had plainly not liked the way Thorgunna stood close to Gerald and spoke for him. Now he fleered and said: 'I might also doubt your skill in fighting.'

'That I have been trained for,' said Gerald grimly.

'Will you wrestle with me?' asked Ketill.

'Gladly!' spat Gerald.

Priest, what is a man to think? As I grow older, I find life to be less and less the good-and-evil, black-and-white thing you call it; we are each of us some hue of gray. This useless fellow, this spiritless lout who could be asked if he did women's work and not lift ax, went out into the yard with Ketill Hjalmarsson and threw him three times running. He had a trick of grabbing the clothes as Ketill rushed on him. . . . I cried a stop when the youth was nearing murderous rage, praised them both, and filled the beer horns. But Ketill brooded sullen on the bench the whole evening.

Gerald said something about making a gun like his own, but bigger, a *cannon* he called it, which could sink ships and scatter hosts. He would need the help of smiths, and also various stuffs. Charcoal was easy and sulfur could be found by the volcanoes, I suppose, but what is this saltpeter?

Too, being wary by now, I questioned him closely as to how he would make such a thing. Did he know just how to mix the powder? No, he admitted. What size must the gun be? When he told me—at least as long as a man—I laughed and asked him how a piece that size could be cast or bored, supposing we could scrape together so much iron. This he did not know either.

'You haven't the tools to make the tools to make the tools,' he said. I don't understand what he meant by that. 'God help me, I can't run through a thousand years of history by myself.'

He took out the last of his little smoke sticks and lit it. Helgi had tried a puff earlier and gotten sick, though he remained a friend of Gerald's. Now my son proposed to take a boat in the morning and go with him and me to Ice Fjord, where I had some money outstanding I wanted to collect. Hjalmar and Ketill said they would come along for the trip, and Thorgunna pleaded so hard that I let her come too.

'An ill thing,' mumbled Sigurd. 'The land-trolls like not a woman aboard a vessel. It's unlucky.'

'How did your fathers bring women to this island?' I grinned.

Now I wish I had listened to him. He was not a clever man, but he often knew whereof he spoke.

At this time I owned a halfshare in a ship that went to Norway, bartering wadmal for timber. It was a profitable business until she ran afoul of vikings during the uproar while Olaf Tryggvason was overthrowing Jarl Haakon there. Some men will do anything to make a living—thieves, cut-throats, they ought to be hanged, the worthless robbers pouncing on honest merchantmen. Had they any courage or honor they would go to Ireland, which is full of plunder.

Well, anyhow, the ship was abroad, but we had three boats and took one of these. Grim went with us others: myself, Helgi, Hjalmar, Ketill, Gerald, and Thorgunna. I saw how the castaway winced at the cold water as we launched her, yet afterward took off his shoes and stockings to let his feet dry. He had been surprised to learn we had a bathhouse—did he think us savages?—but still, he was dainty as a girl and soon moved upwind of our feet.

We had a favoring breeze, so raised mast and sail. Gerald tried to help, but of course did not know one line from another and got them fouled. Grim snarled at him and Ketill laughed nastily. But erelong we were under weigh, and he came and sat by me where I had the steering oar.

He must have lain long awake thinking, for now he ventured shyly: 'In my land they have . . . will have . . . a rig and rudder which are better than these. With them, you can sail so close to the wind that you can crisscross against it.'

'Ah, our wise sailor offers us redes,' sneered Ketill.

'Be still,' said Thorgunna sharply. 'Let Gerald speak.'

Gerald gave her a look of humble thanks, and I was not unwilling to listen. 'This is something which could easily be made,' he said. 'While not a seaman, I've been on such boats myself and know them well. First, then, the sail should not be square and hung from a yardarm, but three-cornered, with the two bottom corners lashed to a yard swiveling fore and aft from the mast; and there should be one or two smaller headsails of the same shape. Next, your steering oar is in the wrong place. You should have a rudder in the stern, guided by a bar.' He grew eager and traced the plan with his fingernail on Thorgunna's cloak. 'With these two things, and a deep keel, going down about three feet for a boat this size, a ship can move across the wind . . . thus.'

Well, priest, I must say the idea has merits, and were it not for the fear of bad luck—for everything of his was unlucky—I might yet play with it. But the drawbacks were clear, and I pointed them out in a reasonable way.

'First and worst,' I said, 'this rudder and deep keel would make it impossible to beach this ship or go up a shallow river. Maybe they have many harbors where you hail from, but here a craft must take what landings she can find, and must be speedily launched if there should be an attack.'

'The keel can be built to draw up into the hull,' he said, 'with a box around so that water can't follow.'

'How would you keep dry rot out of the box?' I answered. 'No, your keel must be fixed, and must be heavy if the ship is not to capsize under so much sail as you have drawn. This means iron or lead, ruinously costly.

'Besides,' I said, 'this mast of yours would be hard to unstep when the wind dropped and oars came out. Furthermore, the sails are the wrong shape to stretch as an awning when one must sleep at sea.'

'The ship could lie out, and you go to land in a small

boat,' he said. 'Also, you could build cabins aboard for shelter.'

'The cabins would get in the way of the oars,' I said, 'unless the ship were hopelessly broad-beamed or else the oarsmen sat below a deck; and while I hear that galley slaves do this in the southlands, free men would never row in such foulness.'

'Must you have oars?' he asked like a very child.

Laughter barked along the hull. The gulls themselves, hovering to starboard where the shore rose dark, cried their scorn.

'Do they have tame winds in the place whence you came?' snorted Hjalmar. 'What happens if you're becalmed—for days, maybe, with provisions running out—'

'You could build a ship big enough to carry many weeks' provisions,' said Gerald.

'If you had the wealth of a king, you might,' said Helgi. 'And such a king's ship, lying helpless on a flat sea, would be swarmed by every viking from here to Jomsborg. As for leaving her out on the water while you make camp, what would you have for shelter, or for defense if you should be trapped ashore?'

Gerald slumped. Thorgunna said to him gently: 'Some folk have no heart to try anything new. I think it's a grand idea.'

He smiled at her, a weary smile, and plucked up the will to say something about a means for finding north in cloudy weather; he said a kind of stone always pointed north when hung from a string. I told him mildly that I would be most interested if he could find me some of this stone; or if he knew where it was to be had, I could ask a trader to fetch me a piece. But this he did not know, and fell silent. Ketill opened his mouth, but got such an edged look from Thorgunna that he shut it again. His face declared what a liar he thought Gerald to be.

The wind turned crank after a while, so we lowered the mast and took to the oars. Gerald was strong and willing, though awkward; however, his hands were so soft that erelong they bled. I offered to let him rest, but he kept doggedly at the work.

Watching him sway back and forth, under the dreary creak of the tholes, the shaft red and wet where he gripped it, I thought much about him. He had done everything wrong which a man could do—thus I imagined then, not knowing the future—and I did not like the way Thorgunna's eyes strayed to him and rested. He was no man for my daughter, landless and penniless and helpless. Yet I could not keep from liking him. Whether his tale was true or only madness, I felt he was honest about it; and surely whatever way by which he came hither was a strange one. I noticed the cuts on his chin from my razor; he had said he was not used to our kind of shaving and would grow a beard. He had tried hard. I wondered how well I would have done, landing alone in this witch country of his dreams, with a gap of forever between me and my home.

Maybe that same wretchedness was what had turned Thorgunna's heart. Women are a kittle breed, priest, and you who have forsworn them belike understand them as well as I who have slept with half a hundred in six different lands. I do not think they even understand themselves. Birth and life and death, those are the great mysteries, which none will ever fathom, and a woman is closer to them than a man.

The ill wind stiffened, the sea grew gray and choppy under low, leaden clouds, and our headway was poor. At sunset we could row no more, but must pull in to a small, unpeopled bay, and make camp as well as could be on the strand.

We had brought firewood and tinder along. Gerald, though staggering with weariness, made himself useful, his sulfury sticks kindling the blaze more easily than flint and steel. Thorgunna set herself to cook our supper. We were not much warded by the boat from a lean, whining wind; her cloak fluttered like wings and her hair blew wild above the streaming flames. It was the time of light nights, the sky a dim, dusky blue, the sea a wrinkled metal sheet, and the land like something risen out of dream mists. We men huddled in our own cloaks, holding numbed hands to the fire and saying little.

I felt some cheer was needed, and ordered a cask of my best and strongest ale broached. An evil Norn made me do that, but no man escapes his weird. Our bellies seemed the more empty now when our noses drank in the sputter of a spitted joint, and the ale went swiftly to our heads. I remember declaiming the death-song of Ragnar Hairybreeks for no other reason than that I felt like declaiming it.

Thorgunna came to stand over Gerald where he sat. I saw how her fingers brushed his hair, ever so lightly, and Ketill Hjalmarsson did too. 'Have they no verses in your land?' she asked.

'Not like yours,' he said, glancing up. Neither of them looked away again. 'We sing rather than chant. I wish I had my *gittar* here—that's a kind of harp.'

'Ah, an Irish bard,' said Hjalmar Broadnose.

I remember strangely well how Gerald smiled, and what he said in his own tongue, though I know not the meaning: *'Only on me mither's side, begorra.'* I suppose it was magic.

'Well, sing for us,' laughed Thorgunna.

'Let me think,' he said. 'I shall have to put it in Norse words for you.' After a little while, still staring at her through the windy gloaming, he began a song. It had a tune I liked, thus:

From this valley they tell me you're leaving.
I will miss your bright eyes and sweet smile.
You will carry the sunshine with you
That has brightened my life all the while. . . .

I don't remember the rest, save that it was not quite seemly.

When he had finished, Hjalmar and Grim went over to see if the meat was done. I spied a glimmer of tears in my daughter's eyes. 'That was a lovely thing,' she said.

Ketill sat straight. The flames splashed his face with wild, running red. A rawness was in his tone: 'Yes, we've

101

found what this fellow can do. Sit about and make pretty songs for the girls. Keep him for that, Ospak.'

Thorgunna whitened, and Helgi clapped hand to sword. Gerald's face darkened and his voice grew thick: 'That was no way to talk. Take it back.'

Ketill rose. 'No,' he said. 'I'll ask no pardon of an idler living off honest yeomen.'

He was raging, but had kept sense enough to shift the insult from my family to Gerald alone. Otherwise he and his father would have had the four of us to deal with. As it was, Gerald stood too, fists knotted at his sides, and said: 'Will you step away from here and settle this?'

'Gladly!' Ketill turned and walked a few yards down the beach, taking his shield from the boat. Gerald followed. Thorgunna stood stricken, then snatched his ax and ran after him.

'Are you going weaponless?' she shrieked.

Gerald stopped, looking dazed. 'I don't want anything like that,' he said. 'Fists—'

Ketill puffed himself up and drew sword. 'No doubt you're used to fighting like thralls in your land,' he said. 'So if you'll crave my pardon, I'll let this matter rest.'

Gerald stood with drooped shoulders. He stared at Thorgunna as if he were blind, as if asking her what to do. She handed him the ax.

'So you want me to kill him?' he whispered.

'Yes,' she answered.

Then I knew she loved him, for otherwise why should she have cared if he disgraced himself?

Helgi brought him his helmet. He put it on, took the ax, and went forward.

'Ill is this,' said Hjalmar to me. 'Do you stand by the stranger, Ospak?'

'No,' I said. 'He's no kin or oath-brother of mine. This is not my quarrel.'

'That's good,' said Hjalmar. 'I'd not like to fight with you. You were ever a good neighbor.'

We stepped forth together and staked out the ground. Thorgunna told me to lend Gerald my sword, so he could use a shield too, but the man looked oddly at me and said he would rather have the ax. They squared off before each other, he and Ketill, and began fighting.

This was no holmgang, with rules and a fixed order of blows and first blood meaning victory. There was death between those two. Drunk though the lot of us were, we saw that and so had not tried to make peace. Ketill stormed in with the sword whistling in his hand. Gerald sprang back, wielding the ax awkwardly. It bounced off Ketill's shield. The youth grinned and cut at Gerald's legs. Blood welled forth to stain the ripped breeches.

What followed was butchery. Gerald had never used a battle-ax before. So it turned in his grasp and he struck with the flat of the head. He would have been hewn down at once had Ketill's sword not been blunted on his helmet and had he not been quick on his feet. Even so, he was erelong lurching with a dozen wounds.

'Stop the fight!' Thorgunna cried, and sped toward them. Helgi caught her arms and forced her back, where she struggled and kicked till Grim must help. I saw grief on my son's face, but a wolfish glee on the carle's.

Ketill's blade came down and slashed Gerald's left hand. He dropped the ax. Ketill snarled and readied to finish him. Gerald drew his gun. It made a flash and a barking noise. Ketill fell. Blood gushed from him. His lower jaw was blown off and the back of his skull was gone.

A stillness came, where only the wind and the sea had voice.

Then Hjalmar trod forth, his mouth working but otherwise a cold steadiness over him. He knelt and closed his son's eyes, as a token that the right of vengeance was his. Rising, he said: 'That was an evil deed. For that you shall be outlawed.'

'It wasn't witchcraft,' said Gerald in a stunned tone. 'It was like a . . . a bow. I had no choice. I didn't want to fight with more than my fists.'

I got between them and said the Thing must decide this matter, but that I hoped Hjalmar would take were-gild for Ketill.

'But I killed him to save my own life!' protested Gerald.

'Nevertheless, weregild must be paid, if Ketill's kin will take it,' I explained. 'Because of the weapon, I think it will be doubled, but that is for the Thing to judge.'

Hjalmar had many other sons, and it was not as if Gerald belonged to a family at odds with his own, so I felt he would agree. However, he laughed coldly and asked where a man lacking wealth would find the silver.

Thorgunna stepped up with a wintry calm and said we would pay. I opened my mouth, but when I saw her eyes I nodded. 'Yes, we will,' I said, 'in order to keep the peace.'

'So you make this quarrel your own?' asked Hjalmar.

'No,' I answered. 'This man is no blood of mine. But if I choose to make him a gift of money to use as he wishes, what of it?'

Hjalmar smiled. Sorrow stood in his gaze, but he looked on me with old comradeship.

'One day he may be your son-in-law,' he said. 'I know the signs, Ospak. Then indeed he will be of your folk. Even helping him now in his need will range you on his side.'

'And so?' asked Helgi, most softly.

'And so, while I value your friendship, I have sons who will take the death of their brother ill. They'll want revenge on Gerald Samsson, if only for the sake of their good names, and thus our two houses will be sundered and one manslaying will lead to another. It has happened often enough ere now.' Hjalmar sighed. 'I myself wish peace with you, Ospak, but if you take this killer's side it must be otherwise.'

I thought for a moment, thought of Helgi lying with his head cloven, of my other sons on their steads drawn to battle because of a man they had never seen, I thought of having to wear byrnies each time we went down for driftwood and never knowing when we went to bed if we would wake to find the house ringed in by spearmen.

'Yes,' I said, 'you are right, Hjalmar. I withdraw my

offer. Let this be a matter between you and him alone.'

We gripped hands on it.

Thorgunna uttered a small cry and flew into Gerald's arms. He held her close. 'What does this mean?' he asked slowly.

'I cannot keep you any longer,' I said, 'but maybe some crofter will give you a roof. Hjalmar is a law-abiding man and will not harm you until the Thing has outlawed you. That will not be before they meet in fall. You can try to get passage out of Iceland ere then.'

'A useless one like me?' he replied in bitterness.

Thorgunna whirled free and blazed that I was a coward and a perjurer and all else evil. I let her have it out before I laid my hands on her shoulders.

'I do this for the house,' I said. 'The house and the blood, which are holy. Men die and women weep, but while the kindred live our names are remembered. Can you ask a score of men to die for your hankerings?'

Long did she stand, and to this day I know not what her answer would have been. But Gerald spoke.

'No,' he said. 'I suppose you have right, Ospak . . . the right of your time, which is not mine.' He took my hand, and Helgi's. His lips brushed Thorgunna's cheek. Then he turned and walked out into the darkness.

I heard, later, that he went to earth with Thorvald Hallsson, the crofter of Humpback Fell, and did not tell his host what had happened. He must have hoped to go unnoticed until he could somehow get berth on an eastbound ship. But of course word spread. I remember his brag that in the United States folk had ways to talk from one end of the land to another. So he must have scoffed at us, sitting in our lonely steads, and not known how fast news would get around. Thorvald's son Hrolf went to Brand Sealskin-Boots to talk about some matter, and mentioned the guest, and soon the whole western island had the tale.

Now, if Gerald had known he must give notice of a man-slaying at the first garth he found, he would have been safe at least till the Thing met, for Hjalmar and his sons are sober men who would not needlessly kill a man still under the wing of the law. But as it was, his keeping the matter secret made him a murderer and therefore at once an outlaw. Hjalmar and his kin rode straight to Humpback Fell and haled him forth. He shot his way past them with the gun and fled into the hills. They followed him, having several hurts and one more death to avenge. I wonder if Gerald thought the strangeness of his weapon would unnerve us. He may not have understood that every man dies when his time comes, neither sooner nor later, so that fear of death is useless.

At the end, when they had him trapped, his weapon gave out on him. Then he took a dead man's sword and defended himself so valiantly that Ulf Hjalmarsson has limped ever since. That was well done, as even his foes admitted. They are an eldritch breed in the United States, but they do not lack manhood.

When he was slain, his body was brought back. For fear of the ghost, he having maybe been a warlock, it was burned, and everything he had owned was laid in the fire with him. Thus I lost the knife he gave me. The barrow stands out on the moor, north of here, and folk shun it, though the ghost has not walked. Today, with so much else happening, he is slowly being forgotten.

And that is the tale, priest, as I saw it and heard it. Most men think Gerald Samsson was crazy, but I myself now believe he did come from out of time, and that his doom was that no man may ripen a field before harvest season. Yet I look into the future, a thousand years hence, when they fly through the air and ride in horseless wagons and smash whole towns with one blow. I think of this Iceland then, and of the young United States men come to help defend us in a year when the end of the world hovers close. Maybe some of them, walking about on the heaths, will see that barrow and wonder what ancient warrior lies buried there, and they may well wish they had lived long ago in his time, when men were free.

Marius

It was raining again, with a bite in the air as the planet spun toward winter. They hadn't yet restored the street lights, and an early dusk seeped up between ruined walls and hid the tattered people who dwelt in caves grubbed out of rubble. Etienne Fourre, chief of the Maquisard Brotherhood and therefore representative of France in the Supreme Council of United Free Europe, stubbed his toe on a cobblestone. Pain struck through a worn-out boot, and he swore with tired expertise. The fifty guards ringing him in, hairy men in a patchwork of clothes—looted from the uniforms of a dozen armies, their own insignia merely a handsewn Tricolor brassard—tensed. That was an automatic reaction, the bristling of a wolf at any unawaited noise, long ago drilled into them.

'Eh, bien,' said Fourre. 'Perhaps Rouget de l'Isle stumbled on the same rock while composing the "Marseillaise."'

One-eyed Astier shrugged, an almost invisible gesture in the murk. 'When is the next grain shipment due?' he asked. It was hard to think of anything but food above the noise of a shrunken belly, and the Liberators had shucked military formalities during the desperate years.

'Tomorrow, I think, or the next day, if the barges aren't waylaid by river pirates,' said Fourre. 'And I don't believe they will be, so close to Strasbourg.' He tried to smile. 'Be of good cheer, my old. Next year should give

107

an ample harvest. The Americans are shipping us a new blight-preventive.'

'Always next year,' grumbled Astier. 'Why don't they send us something to eat now?'

'The blights hit them, too. This is the best they can do for us. Had it not been for them, we would still be skulking in the woods sniping at Russians.'

'We had a little something to do with winning.'

'More than a little, thanks to Professor Valti. I do not think any of our side could have won without all the others.'

'If you call this victory.' Astier's soured voice faded into silence. They were passing the broken cathedral, where childpacks often hid. The little wild ones had sometimes attacked armed men with their jagged bottles and rusty bayonets. But fifty soldiers were too many, of course. Fourre thought he heard a scuttering among the stones; but that might only have been the rats. Never had he dreamed there could be so many rats.

The thin, sad rain blew into his face and weighted his beard. Night rolled out of the east, like a message from Soviet lands plunged into chaos and murder. *But we are rebuilding*, he told himself defensively. Each week the authority of the Strasbourg Council reached a civilizing hand farther into the smashed countries of Europe. In ten years, five perhaps—automation was so fantastically productive, if only you could get hold of the machines in the first place—the men of the West would again be peaceful farmers and shopkeepers, their culture again a going concern.

If the multinational Councillors made the right decisions. And they had not been making them. Valti had finally convinced Fourre of that. Therefore he walked through the rain, hugging an old bicycle poncho to his sleazy jacket, and men in barracks were quietly estimating how many jumps it would take to reach their racked weapons. For they must overpower those who did not agree.

A wry notion, that the feudal principle of personal loyalty to a chief should have to be invoked to enforce the decrees of a new mathematics that only some thousand minds in the world understood. But you wouldn't expect the Norman peasant Astier or the Parisian apache Renault to bend the scanty spare time of a year to learning the operations of symbolic sociology. You would merely say, 'Come,' and they would come because they loved you.

The streets resounded hollow under his feet. It was a world without logic, this one. Only the accidents of survival had made the village apothecary Étienne Fourre into the *de facto* commander of Free France. He could have wished those accidents had taken him and spared Jeanette, but at least he had two sons living, and someday, if they hadn't gotten too much radiation, there would be grandchildren. God was not altogether revengeful.

'There we are, up ahead,' said Astier.

Fourre did not bother to reply. He had never been under the common human necessity of forever mouthing words.

Strasbourg was the seat of the Council because of location and because it was not too badly hit. Only a conventional battle with chemical explosives had rolled through here eighteen months ago. The University was almost unscathed, and so became the headquarters of Jacques Reinach. His men prowled about on guard; one wondered what Goethe would have thought could he have returned to the scene of his student days. And yet it was men such as this, with dirty hands and clean weapons, who were civilization. It was their kind who had harried the wounded Russian colossus out of the West and who would restore law and liberty and wind-rippled fields of grain. Someday. Perhaps.

A machine-gun nest stood at the first checkpoint. The sergeant in charge recognized Fourre and gave a sloppy salute. (Still, the fact that Reinach had imposed so much discipline on his horde spoke for the man's personality.) 'Your escort must wait here, my general,' he said, half apologizing. 'A new regulation.'

'I know,' said Fourre. Not all of his guards did, and he

must shush a snarling. 'I have an appointment with the Commandant.'

'Yes, sir. Please stay to the lighted paths. Otherwise you might be shot by mistake for a looter.'

Fourre nodded and walked through, in among the buildings. His body wanted to get in out of the rain, but he went slowly, delaying the moment. Jacques Reinach was not just his countryman but his friend. Fourre was nowhere near as close to, say, Helgesen of the Nordic Alliance, or the Italian Totti, or Rojansky of Poland, and he positively disliked the German Auerbach.

But Valti's matrices were not concerned with a man's heart. They simply told you that given such and such conditions, this and that would probably happen. It was a cold knowledge to bear.

The structure housing the main offices was a loom of darkness, but a few windows glowed at Fourre. Reinach had had an electric generator installed—and rightly, to be sure, when his tired staff and his tired self must often work around the clock.

A sentry admitted Fourre to an outer room. There half a dozen men picked their teeth and diced for cartridges while a tubercular secretary coughed over files written on old laundry bills, flyleaves, any scrap of paper that came to hand. The lot of them stood up, and Fourre told them he had come to see the Commandant, chairman of the Council.

'Yes, sir.' The officer was still in his teens, fuzzy face already shriveled into old age, and spoke very bad French. 'Check your guns with us and go on in.'

Fourre unbuckled his pistols, reflecting that this latest requirement, the disarming of commanders before they could meet Chairman Reinach, was what had driven Álvarez into fury and the conspiracy. Yet the decree was not unreasonable; Reinach must know of gathering opposition, and everyone had grown far too used to settling disputes violently. Ah, well, Álvarez was no philosopher, but he was boss of the Iberian Irregulars, and you had to use what human material was available.

The officer frisked him, and that was a wholly new

indignity, which heated Fourre's own skin. He choked his anger, thinking that Valti had predicted as much.

Down a corridor then, which smelled moldy in the autumnal dankness, and to a door where one more sentry was posted. Fourre nodded at him and opened the door.

'Good evening, Étienne. What can I do for you?'

The big blond man looked from his desk and smiled. It was a curiously shy, almost a young smile, and something wrenched within Fourre.

This had been a professor's office before the war. Dust lay thick on the books that lined the walls. Really, they should take more care of books, even if it meant giving less attention to famine and plague and banditry. At the rear was a closed window, with a dark wash of rain flowing across miraculously intact glass. Reinach sat with a lamp by his side and his back to the night.

Fourre lowered himself. The visitor's chair creaked under a gaunt-fleshed but heavy-boned weight. 'Can't you guess, Jacques?' he asked.

The handsome Alsatian face, one of the few clean-shaven faces left in the world, turned to study him for a while. 'I wasn't sure you were against me, too,' said Reinach. 'Helgesen, Totti, Alexios . . . yes, that gang . . . but you? We have been friends for many years, Étienne. I didn't expect you would turn on me.'

'Not on you.' Fourre sighed and wished for a cigaret, but tobacco was a remote memory. 'Never you, Jacques. Only your policies. I am here, speaking for all of us—'

'Not quite all,' said Reinach. His tone was quiet and unaccusing. 'Now I realize how cleverly you maneuvered my firm supporters out of town. Brevoort flying off to Ukrainia to establish relations with the revolutionary government; Ferenczi down in Genoa to collect those ships for our merchant marine; Janosek talked into leading an expedition against the bandits in Schleswig. Yes, yes, you plotted this carefully, didn't you? But what do you think they will have to say on their return?'

'They will accept a *fait accompli*,' answered Fourre. 'This generation has had a gutful of war. But I said I was

111

here to speak to you on behalf of my associates. We hoped you would listen to reason from me, at least.'

'If it is reason.' Reinach leaned back in his chair, cat-comfortable, one palm resting on a revolver butt. 'We have threshed out the arguments in council. If you start them again—'

'—it is because I must.' Fourre sat looking at the scarred, bony hands in his lap. 'We do understand, Jacques, that the chairman of the Council must have supreme power for the duration of the emergency. We agreed to give you the final word. But not the *only* word.'

A paleness of anger flicked across the blue eyes. 'I have been maligned enough,' said Reinach coldly. 'They think I want to make myself a dictator. Étienne, after the Second War was over and you went off and became a snug civilian, why do you think I elected to make the Army my career? Not because I had any taste for militarism. But I foresaw our land would again be in danger, within my own lifetime, and I wanted to hold myself ready. Does that sound like . . . like some new kind of Hitler?'

'No, of course not, my friend. You did nothing but follow the example of de Gaulle. And when we chose you to lead our combined forces, we could not have chosen better. Without you—and Valti—there would still be war on the eastern front. We . . . I . . . we think of you as our deliverer, just as if we were the littlest peasant given back his own plot of earth. But you have not been *right*.'

'Everyone makes mistakes.' Reinach actually smiled. 'I admit my own. I bungled badly in cleaning out those Communists at—'

Fourre shook his head stubbornly. 'You don't understand, Jacques. It isn't that kind of mistake I mean. Your great error is that you have not realized we are at peace. The war is over.'

Reinach lifted a sardonic brow. 'Not a barge goes along the Rhine, not a kilometer of railroad track is relaid, but we have to fight bandits, local warlords, half-crazed fanatics of a hundred new breeds. Does that sound like peacetime?'

'It is a difference of . . . of objectives,' said Fourre. 'And man is such an animal that it is the end, not the means, which makes the difference. War is morally simple: one purpose, to impose your will upon the enemy. Not to surrender to an inferior force. But a policeman? He is protecting an entire society, of which the criminal is also a part. A politician? He has to make compromises, even with small groups and with people he despises. You think like a soldier, Jacques, and we no longer want or need a soldier commanding us.'

'Now you're quoting that senile fool Valti,' snapped Reinach.

'If we hadn't had Professor Valti and his sociosymbolic logic to plan our strategy for us we would still be locked with the Russians. There was no way for us to be liberated from the outside this time. The Anglo-Saxon countries had little strength to spare, after the exchange of missiles, and that little had to go to Asia. They could not invade a Europe occupied by a Red Army whose back was against the wall of its own wrecked homeland. We had to liberate ourselves, with ragged men and bicycle cavalry and aircraft patched together out of wrecks. Had it not been for Valti's plans—and, to be sure, your execution of them—we could never have done so.' Fourre shook his head again. He would *not* get angry with Jacques. 'I think such a record entitles the professor to respect.'

'True . . . then.' Reinach's tone lifted and grew rapid. 'But he's senile now, I tell you. Babbling of the future, of long-range trends— Can we eat the future? People are dying of plague and starvation and anarchy now!'

'He has convinced me,' said Fourre. 'I thought much the same as you, myself, a year ago. But he instructed me in the elements of his science, and he showed me the way we are heading. He is an old man, Eino Valti, but a brain still lives under that bald pate.'

Reinach relaxed. Warmth and tolerance played across

113

his lips. 'Very well, Étienne,' he asked, 'what way are we heading?'

Fourre looked past him into night. 'Toward war,' he said, quite softly. 'Another nuclear war, some fifty years hence. It isn't certain the human race can survive that.'

Rain stammered on the windowpanes, falling hard now, and wind hooted in the empty streets. Fourre glanced at his watch. Scant time was left. He fingered the police whistle hung about his neck.

Reinach had started. But gradually he eased back. 'If I thought that were so,' he replied, 'I would resign this minute.'

'I know you would,' mumbled Fourre. 'That is what makes my task so hard for me.'

'However, it isn't so.' Reinach's hand waved as if to brush away a nightmare. 'People have had such a grim lesson that—'

'People, in the mass, don't learn,' Fourre told him. 'Did Germany learn from the Hundred Years' War, or we from Hiroshima? The only way to prevent future wars is to establish a world peace authority: to reconstitute the United Nations and give it some muscles, as well as a charter which favors civilization above any fiction of "equality." And Europe is crucial to that enterprise. North of the Himalayas and east of the Don is nothing any more—howling cannibals. It will take too long to civilize them again. We, ourselves, must speak for the whole Eurasian continent.'

'Very good, very good,' said Reinach impatiently. 'Granted. But what am I doing that is wrong?'

'A great many things, Jacques. You have heard about them in the Council. Need I repeat the long list?' Fourre's head turned slowly, as if it creaked on its neckbones, and locked eyes with the man behind the desk. 'It is one thing to improvise in wartime. But you are improvising the peace. You forced the decision to send only two men to represent our combined nations at the conference planned in Rio. Why? Because we're short on transportation, clerical help, paper, even on decent clothes! The problem should have been studied. It may

114

be all right to treat Europe as a unit—or it may not; perhaps this will actually exacerbate nationalism. You made the decision in one minute when the question was raised, and would not hear debate.'

'Of course not,' said Reinach harshly. 'If you remember, that was the day we learned of the neofasicst coup in Corsica.'

'Corsica could have waited awhile. The place would have been more difficult to win back, yes, if we hadn't struck at once. But this business of our U. N. representation could decide the entire future of—'

'I know, I know. Valti and his theory about the "pivotal decision." Bah!'

'The theory happens to work, my old.'

'Within proper limits. I'm a hard head, Étienne, I admit that.' Reinach leaned across the desk, chuckling. 'Don't you think the times demand a hard head? When hell is romping loose, it's no time to spin find philosophies . . . or try to elect a parliament, which I understand is another of the postponements Dr. Valti holds against me.'

'It is,' said Fourre. 'Do you like roses?'

'Why, why . . . yes.' Reinach blinked. 'To look at, anyway.' Wistfulness crossed his eyes. 'Now that you mention it, it's been many years since I last saw a rose.'

'But you don't like gardening. I remember that from, from old days.' The curious tenderness of man for man, which no one has ever quite explained, tugged at Fourre. He cast it aside, not daring to do otherwise, and said impersonally: 'And you like democratic government, too, but were never interested in the grubby work of maintaining it. There is a time to plant seeds. If we delay we will be too late; strong-arm rule will have become too ingrained a habit.'

'There is also a time to keep alive. Just to keep alive, nothing else.'

'Jacques, I don't accuse you of hardheartedness. You are a sentimentalist: you see a child with belly bloated from hunger, a house marked with a cross to show that the Black Death has walked in—and you feel too much pity to be able to think. It is . . . Valti, myself, the rest of us . . . who are cold-blooded, who are prepared to sacrifice a few thousand more lives now, by neglecting the immediately necessary, for the sake of saving all humankind fifty years hence.'

'You may be right,' said Reinach. 'About your cold souls, I mean.' His voice was so low that the rain nearly drowned it.

Fourre stole another look at his watch. This was taking longer than expected. He said in a slurred, hurried tone: 'What touched off tonight's affair was the Pappas business.'

'I thought so,' agreed Reinach evenly. 'I don't like it either. I know as well as you do that Pappas is a murderous crypto-Communist scoundrel whose own people hate him. But curse it, man, don't you know rats do worse than steal food and gnaw the faces of sleeping children? Don't you know they spread plague? And Pappas has offered us the services of the only efficient rat-exterminating force in Eurasia. He asks nothing in return except that we recognize his Macedonian Free State and give him a seat on the Council.'

'Too high a price,' said Fourre. 'In two or three years we can bring the rats under control ourselves.'

'And meanwhile?'

'Meanwhile, we must hope that nobody we love is taken sick.'

Reinach grinned without mirth. 'It won't do,' he said. 'I can't agree to that. If Pappas' squads help us, we can save a year of reconstruction, a hundred thousand lives—'

'And throw away lives by the hundred millions in the future.'

'Oh, come now. One little province like Macedonia?'

'One very big precedent,' said Fourre. 'We will not merely be conceding a petty warlord the right to his loot. We will be conceding—he lifted furry hands and counted off on the fingers—'the right of any ideological dictatorship, anywhere, to exist: which right, if yielded, means war and war and war again; the fatally outmoded principle of unlimited national sovereignty; the friend-

116

ship of an outraged Greece, which is sure to invoke that same principle in retaliation; the inevitable political repercussions throughout the near East, which is already turbulent enough; therefore war between us and the Arabs, because we *must* have oil; a seat on the Council to a clever and ruthless man who, frankly, Jacques, can think rings around you— No!'

'You are theorizing about tomorrow,' said Reinach. 'The rats are already here. What would you have me do instead?'

'Refuse the offer. Let me take a brigade down there. We can knock Pappas to hell . . . unless we let him get too strong first.'

Reinach shook his head good-naturedly. 'Who's the warmonger now?' he said with a laugh.

'I never denied we still have a great deal of fighting ahead of us,' Fourre said. Sadness tinged his voice; he had seen too many men spilling their guts on the ground and screaming. 'I only want to be sure it will serve the final purpose, that there shall never again be a world war. That my children and grandchildren will not have to fight at all.'

'And Valti's equations show the way to achieve that?' Reinach asked quietly.

'Well, they show how to make the outcome reasonably probable.'

'I'm sorry, Étienne.' Reinach shook his head. 'I simply cannot believe that. Turning human society into a . . . what's the word? . . . a potential field, and operating on it with symbolic logic: it's too remote. I am here, in the flesh—such of it as is left, on our diet—not in a set of scribbles made by some band of long-haired theorists.'

'A similar band discovered atomic energy,' said Fourre. 'Yes, Valti's science is young. But within admitted limitations, it works. If you would just study—'

'I have too much else on hand.' Reinach shrugged. A blankness drew across his face. 'We've wasted more time than I can afford already. What does your group of generals want me to do?'

Fourre gave it to him as he knew his comrade would

wish it, hard and straight like a bayonet thrust. 'We ask for your resignation. Naturally, you'll keep a seat on the Council, but Professor Valti will assume the chairmanship and set about making the reforms we want. We will issue a formal promise to hold a constitutional convention in the spring and dissolve the military government within one year.'

He bent his head and looked at the time. A minute and a half remained.

'No,' said Reinach.

'But—'

'Be still!' The Alsatian stood up. The single lamp threw his shadow grotesque and enormous across the dusty books. 'Do you think I didn't see this coming? Why do you imagine I let only one man at a time in here, and disarm him? The devil with your generals! The common people know me, they know I stand for them first—and hell take your misty futures! We'll meet the future when it gets here.'

'That is what man has always done,' said Fourre. He spoke like a beggar. 'And that is why the race has always blundered from one catastrophe to the next. This may be our last chance to change the pattern.'

Reinach began pacing back and forth behind his desk. 'Do you think I like this miserable job?' he retorted. 'It simply happens that no one else can do it.'

'So now you are the indispensable man,' whispered Fourre. 'I had hoped you would escape that.'

'Go on home, Étienne.' Reinach halted, and kindness returned to him. 'Go back and tell them I won't hold this against them personally. You had a right to make your demand. Well, it has been made and refused.' He nodded to himself thoughtfully. 'We will have to make some change in our organization, though. I don't want to be a dictator, but—'

Zero hour. Fourre felt very tired.

He had been denied, and so he had not blown the whistle that would stop the rebels, and matters were out of his hands now.

'Sit down,' he said. 'Sit down, Marius, and let us talk about old times for a while.'

Reinach looked surprised. 'Marius? What do you mean?'

'Oh . . . an example from history which Professor Valti gave me.' Fourre considered the floor. There was a cracked board by his left foot. Cracked and crazy, a tottering wreck of a civilization, how had the same race built Chartres and the hydrogen bomb?

His words dragged out of him: 'In the second century before Christ, the Cimbri and their allies, Teutonic barbarians, came down out of the north. For a generation they wandered about, ripping Europe apart. They chopped to pieces the Roman armies sent to stop them. Finally they invaded Italy. It did not look as if they could be halted before they took Rome herself. But one general by the name of Marius rallied his men. He met the barbarians and annihilated them.'

'Why, thank you.' Reinach sat down, puzzled. 'But—'

'Never mind.' Fourre's lips twisted into a smile. 'Let us take a few minutes free and just talk. Do you remember that night soon after the Second War, we were boys freshly out of the Maquis, and we tumbled around the streets of Paris and toasted the sunrise from Sacré Coeur?'

'Yes. To be sure. That was a wild night!' Reinach laughed. 'How long ago it seems. What was your girl's name? I've forgotten.'

'Marie. And you had Simone. A beautiful little baggage, Simone. I wonder whatever became of her.'

'I don't know. The last I heard—No. Remember how bewildered the waiter was when—'

A shot cracked through the rain, and then the wrathful clatter of machine guns awoke. Reinach was on his feet in one tiger bound, pistol in hand, crouched by the window. Fourre stayed seated.

The noise lifted, louder and closer. Reinach spun about. His gun muzzle glared emptily at Fourre.

'Yes, Jacques.'

119

'*Mutiny!*'

'We had to.' Fourre discovered that he could again meet Reinach's eyes. 'The situation was that crucial. If you had yielded . . . if you had even been willing to discuss the question . . . I would have blown this whistle and nothing would have happened. Now we're too late, unless you want to surrender. If you do, our offer still stands. We will want you to work with us.'

A grenade blasted somewhere nearby.

'You—'

'Go on and shoot. It doesn't matter very much.'

'No.' The pistol wavered. 'Not unless you— Stay where you are! Don't move!' The hand Reinach passed across his forehead shuddered. 'You know how well this place is guarded. You know the people will rise to my side.'

'I think not. They worship you, yes, but they are tired and starved. Just in case, though, we staged this for the nighttime. By tomorrow morning the business will be over.' Fourre spoke like a rusty engine. 'The barracks have already been seized. Those more distant noises are the artillery being captured. The University is surrounded, and cannot stand against an attack.'

'This building can.'

'So you won't quit, Jacques?'

'If I could do that,' said Reinach, 'I wouldn't be here tonight.'

The window broke open. Reinach whirled. The man who was vaulting through shot first.

The sentry outside the door looked in. His rifle was poised, but he died before he could use it. Men with black clothes and blackened faces swarmed across the sill.

Fourre knelt beside Reinach. A bullet through the head had been quick, at least. But if it had struck further down, perhaps Reinach's life could have been saved. Fourre wanted to weep, but he had forgotten how.

The big man who had killed Reinach ignored his commandos to stoop over the body with Fourre. 'I'm sorry, sir,' he whispered. It was hard to tell whom he spoke to.

'Not your fault, Stefan.' Fourre's voice jerked.

'We had to run through the shadows, get under the wall. I got a boost through this window. Didn't have time to take aim. I didn't realize who he was till—'

'It's all right, I said. Go on, now, take charge of your party, get this building cleaned out. Once we hold it, the rest of his partisans should yield pretty soon.'

The big man nodded and went out into the corridor.

Fourre crouched by Jacques Reinach while a sleet of bullets drummed on the outer walls. He heard them only dimly. Most of him was wondering if this hadn't been the best ending. Now they could give their chief a funeral with full military honors, and later they would build a monument to the man who saved the West, and—

And it might not be quite that easy to bribe a ghost. But you had to try.

'I didn't tell you the whole story, Jacques,' he said. His hands were like a stranger's, using his jacket to wipe off the blood, and his words ran on of themselves. 'I wish I had. Maybe you would have understood . . . and maybe not. Marius went into politics afterward, you see. He had the prestige of his victory behind him, he was the most powerful man in Rome, his intentions were noble, but he did not understand politics. There followed a witch's dance of corruption, murder, civil war, fifty years of it, the final extinction of the Republic. Caesarism merely gave a name to what had already been done.

'I would like to think that I helped spare Jacques Reinach the name of Marius.'

Rain slanted in through the broken window. Fourre reached out and closed the darkened eyes. He wondered if he would ever be able to close them within himself.

Progress

1

'There they are! Aircraft ho-o-o!'

Keanua's bull bellow came faintly down to Ranu from the crow's nest, almost drowned in the slatting and cracking of sails. He could have spoken clearly head-to-head, but best save that for real emergencies. Otherwise, by some accident, the Brahmards might learn about it.

If they don't already know, Ranu thought.

The day was too bright for what was going to happen. Big, wrinkled waves marched past. Their backs were a hundred different blues, from the color of the sky overhead to a royal midnight; their troughs shaded through gray-amber to a clear green. Foam swirled intricately upon them. Further off they became a single restlessness that glittered with sunlight, on out to the horizon. They rushed and rumbled, they smacked against the hulls, which rolled somewhat beneath Ranu's feet, making him aware of the interplay in his leg muscles. The air was mild, but had a strong thrust and saltiness to it.

Ranu wished he could sink into the day. Nothing would happen for minutes yet. He should think only about sunlight warming his skin, wind ruffling his hair, blue shadows upon an amazingly white cloud high up where the air was not so swift. Once the Beneghalis arrived, he might be dead. Keanua, he felt sure, wasn't worrying about that until the time came. But then, Keanua was from Taiiti. Ranu had been born and bred in N'Zealann; his Maurai genes were too mixed with the old fretful Ingliss. It showed on his body also, tall and lean, with narrow face and beaky nose, brown hair and the rarity of blue eyes.

He unslung his binoculars and peered after the airship. A light touch on his arm recalled him. He lowered the glasses and smiled lopsidedly at Alisabeta Kanukauai.

'Still too far to see from here,' he told her. 'The topmasts get in the way. But don't bother going aloft. She'll be overhead before you could swarm halfway up the shrouds.'

The wahine nodded. She was rather short, a trifle on the stocky side, but because she was young her figure looked good in the brief lap-lap. A hibiscus flower from the deck garden adorned her blue-black locks, which were cut off just below the ears like the men's. Sailors couldn't be bothered with glamorous tresses, even on a trimaran as broad and stable as this. On some ships, of course, a woman had no duties beyond housekeeping. But Alisabeta was a cyberneticist. The Lohannaso Shippers' Association, to which she and Ranu were both related by blood, preferred to minimize crews; so everybody doubled as something else.

That was one reason the *Aorangi* had been picked for this task. The fact of Alisabeta's technical training could not be hidden from the Brahmards. Eyes sharpened by suspicion would see a thousand subtle traces in her manner, left by years of mathematical logic, physics, engineering. But such would be quite natural in a Lohannaso girl.

Moreover, if this job went sour, only three lives would have been sacrificed. Some merchant craft had as many as ten kanakas and three wahines aboard.

'I suppose I'd better get back to the radio,' said Alisabeta. 'They may want to call.'

'I doubt that,' said Ranu, 'If they aren't simply going to attack us from above, they'll board. They told us they would, when we talked before. But yes, I suppose you had better stand by.'

His gaze followed her with considerable pleasure. Usually, in the culture of the Sea People, there was something a little unnatural about a career woman, a female to whom her own home and children were merely incidental if she elected to have them at all. But Alisabeta had been as good a cook, as merry a companion, as much alive in a man's arms on moonlit nights, as any seventeen-year-old signed on to see the world before she settled down. And she was a damned interesting talk-friend, too. Her interpretations of the shady ethnopolitical situation were so shrewd you might have thought her formally educated in psychodynamics.

I wonder, Ranu said to himself slowly, not for the first time. *Marriage could perhaps work out. It's almost unheard of for a sailor, even a skipper, to have a private woman along. And children. . . . But it has been done, once in a while.*

She vanished behind the carved porch screen of the radio shack, on whose vermin-proofed thatch a bougainvillea twined and flared with color. Ranu jerked his mind back to the present. *Time enough to make personal plans if we get out of this alive.*

The airship hove into view. The shark-shaped gasbag was easily a hundred meters long, the control fins spread out like roc's wings. Propeller noise came softly down through the wind. On the flanks was painted the golden Siva symbol of the Brahmard scientocracy: destruction and rebirth.

Rebirth of what? Well, that's what we're here to learn.

The *Aorangi* was drifting before the wind, but not very fast, with her sails and vanes skewed at such lunatic angles. The aircraft paced her easily, losing altitude until it was hardly above deck level, twenty meters away. Ranu saw turbaned heads and high-collared tunics lining the starboard observation verandah. Keanua, who had scrambled down from the crow's nest, hurried to the port rail and placed himself by one of the cargo-loading king posts. He pulled off his shirt—even a Taiitian needed protection against this tropical sea glare, above the shade of the sails—and waved it to attract attention.

Ranu saw a man on the flyer nod and issue instructions.

Keanua worked the emergency handwheels. A boom swung out. A catapult in the bow of the airship fired a grapnel. That gunner was good; the hook engaged the cargo sling on the first try. It had two lines attached. Keanua—a thick man with elaborate tattoos on his flat cheerful face—brought the grapnel inboard and made one cable fast. He carried the other one aft and secured it to a bollard at the next king post. With the help of the airship's stern catapult he repeated this process in reverse. The two craft were linked.

For a minute the Beneghali pilot got careless and let the cables draw taut. The *Aorangi* heeled with the drag on her. Sails thundered overhead. Ranu winced at the thought of the stresses imposed on his masts and yards. Ship timber wasn't exactly cheap, even after centuries of good forest management. (Briefly and stingingly he recalled those forests, rustling leaves, sunflecked shadows, a glade that suddenly opened on an enormous vista of downs and grazing sheep and one white waterfall: his father's home.) The aircraft was far less able to take such treatment, and the pilot made haste to adjust its position.

When the configuration was balanced, with the Beneghali vessel several meters aloft, a dozen men slid down a cable. The first came in a bosun's chair arrangement, but the others just wrapped an arm and leg around the line. Each free hand carried a weapon.

Ranu crossed the deck to meet them. The leader got out of the chair with dignity. He was not tall, but he held himself straight as a rifle barrel. Trousers, tunic, turban were like snow under the sun. His face was sharp, with tight lips in a grizzled beard. He bowed stiffly. 'At your service, Captain,' he said in the Beneghali version of Hinji. 'Scientist-administrator Indravarman Dhananda makes you welcome to these waters.' The tone was flat.

Ranu refrained from offering a handshake in the manner of the Maurai Federation. 'Captain Ranu Karelo Makintairu,' he said. Like many sailors, he spoke fluent Hinji. His companions had acquired the language in a

126

few weeks' intensive training. They approached, and Ranu introduced them. 'Aeromotive engineer Keanua Filipoa Jouberti; cyberneticist Alisabeta Kanukauai.'

Dhananda's black eyes darted about. 'Are there others?' he asked.

'No,' grunted Keanua. 'We wouldn't be in this pickle if we had some extra hands.'

The bearded, green-uniformed soldiers had quietly moved to command the whole deck. Some stood where they could see no one lurked behind the cabins. They wasted no admiration on grain of wood, screens of Okkaidan shoji, or the strong curve of the roofs. This was an inhumanly businesslike civilization. Ranu noted that besides swords and telescoping pikes, they had two submachine guns.

Yes, he thought with a little chill under his scalp, *Federation Intelligence made no mistake. Something very big indeed is hidden on that island.*

Dhananda ceased studying him. It was obvious that the scantily clad Maurai bore no weapons other than their knives. 'You will forgive our seeming distrustfulness, Captain,' the Brahmard said. 'But the Buruma coast is still infested with pirates.'

'I know.' Ranu made his features smile. 'You see the customary armament emplacements on our deck.'

'Er . . . I understand from your radio call that you are in distress.'

'Considerable,' said Alisabeta. 'Our engine is disabled. Three people cannot possibly trim those sails, and resetting the vanes won't help much.'

'What about dropping the sails and going on propellers?' asked Dhananda. His coldness returned. In Beneghal, only women for hire—a curious institution the Maurai knew almost nothing about—traveled freely with men.

'The screws run off the same engine, sir,' Alisabeta answered, more demurely than before.

'Well, you can let most of the sails fall, can't you, and stop this drift toward the reefs?'

'Not without smashing our superstructure,' Ranu told

him. 'Synthetic or not, that fabric has a lot of total area. It's *heavy*. Worse, it'd be blown around the decks, fouling gear and breaking cabins. Also, we'd still have extremely poor control.' He pointed at the steering wheel aft in the pilothouse, now lashed in place. 'The whole rudder system on craft of this type is based on sail and vane adjustment. For instance, with the wind abeam like this, we ought to strip the mainmast and raise the *wanaroa*—oh, never mind. It's a specially curve-battened, semitubular sail with vanes on its yard to redirect airflow aloft. These trimarans have shallow draft and skimpy keel. It makes them fast, but requires exact rigging.'

'Mmmm . . . yes, I think I understand.' Dhananda tugged his beard and brooded. "What do you need to make you seaworthy again?'

'A dock and a few days to work,' said Alisabeta promptly. 'With your help, we should be able to make Port Arberta.'

'Um-m-m. There are certain difficulties about that. Could you not get a tow on to the mainland from some other vessel?'

'Not in time,' said Ranu. He pointed east, where a shadow lay on the horizon. 'We'll be aground in a few more hours if something isn't done.'

'You know how little trade comes on this route at this season,' Alisabeta added. 'Yours was the only response to our SOS, except for a ship near the Nicbars.' She paused before continuing with what Ranu hoped was not overdone casualness: 'That ship promised to inform our Association of our whereabouts. Her captain assumed a Beneghali patrol would help us put into Arberta for repairs.'

She was not being altogether untruthful. Ships did lie at Car Nicbar—camouflaged sea and aircraft, waiting. But they were hours distant.

Dhananda was not silent long. Whatever decision the Brahmard had made, it came with a swiftness and firmness that Ranu admired. (Though such qualities were not to be wished for in an enemy, were they?) 'Very well,' he yielded, rather sourly. 'We shall assist you into harbor and see that the necessary work is completed.

You can also radio the mainland that you will be late. Where are you bound?'

'Calcut,' said Ranu. 'Wool, hides, preserved fish, timber, and algal oils.'

'You are from N'Zealann, then,' Dhananda concluded.

'Yes. Wellantoa registry. Uh, I'm being inhospitable. Can we not offer the honorable scientist refreshment?'

'Later. Let us get started first.'

That took an hour or so. The Beneghalis were landlubbers. But they could pull strongly on a line at Keanua's direction. So the plasticloth was lowered, slowly and awkwardly, folded and stowed. A couple of studding sails and jibs were left up, a spanker and flowsail were raised, the vanes were adjusted, and the ship began responding somewhat to her rudder. The aircraft paced alongside, still attached. It was far too lightly built, of wicker and fabric, to serve as a drogue; but it helped modify the wind pattern. With her crabwise motion toward the reefs halted, the *Aorangi* limped landward.

Ranu took Dhananda on a guided tour. Few Hinjan countries carried an ocean-borne trade. Their merchants went overland by camel caravan or sent high-priced perishables by air. The Brahmard had never been aboard one of the great vessels that bound together the Maurai Federation, from Awaii in the west to N'Zealann in the south, and carried the Cross and Stars flag around the planet. He was clearly looking for concealed weapons and spies in the woodwork. But he was also interested in the ship for her own sake.

'I am used to schooners and junks and the like,' he said. 'This looks radical.'

'It's a rather new design,' Ranu agreed. 'But more are being built. You'll see many in the future.'

With most sails down, the deck had taken on an austere appearance. Only the cabins, the hatches and king posts, cleats and bollards and defense installations, the sunpower collectors forward, and Keanua's flower garden broke that wide sweep. The three hulls were hidden beneath it, except where the prows jutted forth, bearing extravagantly carved tiki figureheads. There were three masts. Those fore and aft were more or less conventional; the mainmast was a tripod, wrought to withstand tremendous forces. Dhananda admitted he was bewildered by the variety of yards and lines hanging against the sky.

'We trim exactly, according to wind and current,' Ranu explained. 'Continuous measurements are taken by automatic instruments. A computer below decks calculates what's necessary, and directs the engine in the work.'

'I know areodynamics and hydrodynamics are thoroughly developed disciplines,' the Beneghali said, impressed. 'Large modern aircraft couldn't move about on such relatively feeble motors as they have unless they were designed with great care. But I had not appreciated the extent to which the same principles are being applied to marine architecture.' He sighed. 'That is one basic trouble with the world today, Captain. Miserably slow communications. Yes, one can send a radio signal, or cross the ocean in days if the weather is favorable. But so few people do it. The volume of talk and traffic is so small. An invention like this ship can exist for decades before anyone outside its own country is really aware of it. The benefits are denied to more remote people for . . . generations, sometimes.'

He seemed to recognize the intensity that had crept into his voice, and broke off.

'Oh, I don't know,' said Ranu. 'International improvement does go on. Two hundred years ago, say, my ancestors were fooling around with multi-masted hermaphrodite craft, and the Mericans used sails and fan keels on their blimps—with no anticatalyst for the hydrogen! Can you imagine such a firetrap? At the same time, if you'll pardon my saying so, the Hinjan subcontinent was a howling chaos of folk migrations. You couldn't have used even those square-rigger blimps, if someone had offered them to you.'

'What has that to do with my remarks?' Dhananda asked, bridling.

'Just that I believe the Maurai government is right in advocating that the world go slow in making changes,' said Ranu. He was being deliberately provocative, hoping to get a hint of how far things had gone on South Annaman. But Dhananda only shrugged, the dark face congealed into a mask.

'I would like to see your engine,' said the Brahmard.

'This way, then. It's no different in principle from your airship motor, though: just bigger. Runs off dielectric accumulators. Of course, on a surface ship we have room to carry solar collectors and thus recharge our own system.'

'I am surprised that you do not dispense with sails and drive the ship with propellers.'

'We do, but only in emergencies. After all, sunlight is not a particularly concentrated energy source. We'd soon exhaust our accumulators if we made them move us at anything like a decent speed. Not even the newest type of fuel cells have capacity enough. As for that indirect form of sunpower storage known as organic fuel . . . well, we have the same problem in the Islands as you do on the continents. Oil, wood, peat, and coal are too expensive for commercial use. But we find the wind quite satisfactory. Except, to be sure, when the engine breaks down and we can't handle our sails! Then I could wish I were on a nice old-fashioned schooner, not this big, proud, thirty-knot tripler.'

'What happened to your engine, anyhow?'

'A freak accident. A defective rotor, operating at high speed, threw a bearing exactly right to break a winding line. I suppose you know that armatures are usually wound with ceramic tubing impregnated with a conductive solution. This in turn shorted out everything else. The damage is reparable. If we'd had ample sea room, we wouldn't have bothered with that SOS.' Ranu tried to laugh. 'That's why humans are aboard, you know. Theoretically, our computer could be built to do everything. But in practice, something always happens that requires a brain that can think.'

'A computer could be built to do that, too,' said Dhananda.

'But could it be built to give a damn?' Ranu muttered in his own language. As he started down a ladder, one of the soldiers came between him and the sun, so that he felt the shadow of a pike across his back.

2

For centuries after the War of Judgment, the Annaman Islands lay deserted. Their natives regressed easily to a savage state, and took the few outside settlers along. The jungle soon reclaimed those towns the Ingliss had built in their own day. But eventually the outside world recovered somewhat. With its mixed Hinji-Tamil-Paki population firmly under the control of the Udayana Raj, Beneghal accumulated sufficient resources to send out an occasional ship for exploration and trade. A garrison was established on South Annaman. Then the Maurai came. Their more efficient vessels soon dominated seaborne traffic. Nonetheless, Beneghal maintained its claim to the islands. The outpost grew into Port Arberta—which, however, remained small and sleepy, seldom visited by foreign craft.

After the Scientistic Revolution in Beneghal put the Brahmards in power, those idealistic oligarchs tried to start an agricultural colony nearby. But the death rate was infamous, and the project was soon discontinued. Since then, as far as the world knew, there had been nothing more important here than a meteorological station.

But the world didn't know much, Ranu reflected.

He and his companions followed the Beneghalis ashore. The wharf lay bare and bleached in the evening light. A few concrete warehouses stood with empty windows. Some primitive fisher boats had obviously lain docked, unused, for months. Beyond the waterfront, palm-thatched huts straggled up from the bay. Ranked trees bespoke a plantation on the other side of the village. Then the jungle began, solid green on the hills, which

132

rose inland in tiers until their ridges gloomed against the purpling east.

How quiet it was! The villagers had come on the run when they sighted the great ship. They stood massed and staring, several hundred of them—native Annamanese or half-breeds, with black skins and tufty hair and large shy eyes, clad in little more than loincloths. The mainland soldiers towered over them; the Maurai were veritable giants. They should have been swarming about, these people, chattering, shouting, giggling, hustling their wares, the potbellied children clamoring for sweets. But they only stared.

Keanua asked bluntly, 'What ails these folk? We aren't going to eat them.'

'They are afraid of strangers,' Dhananda replied. 'Slave raiders used to come here.'

But that was ended fifty years ago, Ranu thought. *No, any xenophobia they have now is due to rather more recent indoctrination.*

'Besides,' the Brahmard went on pointedly, 'is it not Maurai doctrine that no culture has the right to meddle with the customs of any other?'

Alisabeta winced. 'Yes,' she said.

Dhananda made a surface smile. 'I am afraid you will find our hospitality somewhat limited here. We haven't many facilities for entertainment.'

Ranu looked to his right, past the village, where a steep bluff upheaved itself. On the crest he saw the wooden latticework supporting a radio transmitter—chiefly for the use of the weather observers—and some new construction, bungalows and hangars around an airstrip. The earth scars were not entirely healed; this was hardly more than two or three years old. 'You seem to be expanding,' he remarked with purposeful naïveté.

'Yes, yes,' said Dhananda. 'Our government still hopes to civilize these islands and open them to extensive cultivation. Everyone knows that the Beneghali mainland population is bulging at the seams. But first we must study conditions. Not only the physical environment which defeated our earlier attempt, but the inland tribes.

133

We want to treat them fairly; but what does that mean in their own terms? The old intercultural problem. So we have scientific teams here, making studies.'

'I see.' As she walked toward a waiting donkey cart, Alisabeta studied the villagers with practical sympathy. Ranu, who had encountered many odd folk around the world, believed he could make the same estimate as she. The little dark people were not undernourished, although their fishers had not put out to sea for a long time. They did not watch the Beneghalis as peasants watch tyrants. Rather, there was unease in the looks they gave the Maurai.

Water lapped in the bay. A gull mewed, cruising about with sunlight golden upon its wings. Otherwise the silence grew enormous. It continued after the donkey trotted off, followed by hundreds of eyes. When the graveled road came up where the airfield was, a number of Beneghalis emerged from the houses to watch. They stood on their verandahs with the same withdrawn suspiciousness as the islanders.

The stillness was broken by a roar. A man came bounding down the steps of the largest house and across the field. He was as tall as Ranu and as broad as Keanua, dressed in kilt and blouse, his hair and moustache lurid yellow against a boiled-lobster complexion. A Merican! Ranu stiffened. He saw Alisabeta's fist clench on her knee. Their driver halted the cart.

'Hoy! Welcome! Dhananda, why in Oktai's name didn't you tell me company was coming?'

The Brahmard looked furious. 'We have just gotten here,' he answered in a strained voice. 'I thought you were—' He broke off.

'At the laboratory for the rest of this week?' the Merican boomed. 'Oh yes, so I was, till I heard a foreign ship was approaching the harbor. One of your lads here was talking on the radiophone with our place, asking about our supplies or something. He mentioned it. I overheard. Commandeered an aircraft the first thing. Why didn't you let me know? Welcome, you!' He reached a huge paw across the lap of Dhananda, who sat tense, and engulfed Ranu's hand.

'Lorn's the name,' he said. 'Lorn sunna Browen, of Corado University—and, with all due respect to my good Brahmard colleagues, sick for the sight of a new face. You're Maurai, of course. N'Zealanners, I'd guess. Right?'

He had been a major piece of jigsaw puzzle that Federation Intelligence had fitted together. Relations between the Sea People and the clans of southwest Merica remained fairly close, however little direct trade went on. After all, missions from Awaii had originally turned those aerial pirates to more peaceable ways. Moreover, despite the slowness and thinness of global communications, an international scientific community did exist. So the Maurai professors had been able to nod confidently and say, yes, that Lorn fellow in Corado is probably the world's leading astrophysicist, and the Brahmards wouldn't hire him for no reason.

But there was nothing furtive about him, Ranu saw. He was genuinely delighted to have visitors.

The Maurai introduced themselves. Lorn jogged alongside the cart, burbling like a cataract. 'What, Dhananda, you were going to put them up in that lousy dâk? Nothing doing! I've got my own place here, and plenty of spare room. No, no, Cap'n Ranu, don't bother about thanks. The pleasure is mine. You can show me around your boat if you want to. I'd be interested in that.'

'Certainly,' said Alisabeta. She gave him her best smile. 'Though isn't that a little out of your field?'

Ranu jerked in alarm. But it was Keanua's growl which sounded in their brains: *'Hoai, there, be careful! We're supposed to be plain merchant seamen, remember? We never heard of this Lorn man.'*

'I'm sorry!' Her brown eyes widened in dismay. *'I forgot.'*

'Amateurs, the bunch of us,' Ranu groaned. *'Let's hope our happy comrade Dhananda is just as inept. But I'm afraid he isn't.'*

The Brahmard was watching them keenly. 'Why, what do you think the honorable Lorn's work is?' he asked.

135

'Something to do with your geographical research project,' said Alisabeta. 'What else?' She cocked her head and pursed her lips. 'Now, let me see if I can guess. The Mericans are famous for dry farming . . . but this climate is anything except dry. They are also especially good at mining and ore processing. Ah, hah! You've found heavy-metal deposits in the jungle and aren't letting on.'

Lorn, who had grown embarrassed under Dhananda's glare, cleared his throat and said with false heartiness: 'Well, now, we don't want news to get around too fast, you understand? Spring a surprise on the mercantile world, eh?'

'Best leave the explanations to me, honorable sir.' Dhananda's words fell like lumps of stone. The two soldiers accompanying the party in the cart hefted their scabbarded swords. Lorn glowered and clapped a hand to his broad clansman's dagger.

The moment passed. The cart stopped before a long white bungalow. Servants—mainlanders who walked like men better accustomed to uniforms than livery—took the guests' baggage and bowed them in. They were given adjoining bedrooms, comfortably furnished in the ornate upper-class Hinji style. Since he knew his stuff would be searched anyway, Ranu let a valet help him change into a formal shirt and sarong. But he kept his knife. That was against modern custom, when bandits and barbarians were no longer quite so likely to come down the chimney. Nonetheless, Ranu was not going to let this knife out of his possession.

The short tropic twilight was upon them when they gathered on the verandah for drinks. Dhananda sat in a corner, nursing a glass of something nonalcoholic. Ranu supposed the Brahmard—obviously the security chief here—had pulled rank on Lorn and insisted on being invited to eat. The Maurai skipper stretched out in a wicker chair with Keanua on his left, Alisabeta on his right, Lorn confronting them.

Darkness closed in, deep and blue. The sea glimmered below; the land lay black, humping up toward stars that

136

one by one trod brilliantly forth. Yellow candlelight spilled from windows where the dinner table was being set. Bats darted on the fringe of sight. A lizard scuttled in the thatch overhead. From the jungle came sounds of wild pigs grunting, the scream of a startled peacock, numberless insect chirps. Coolness descended layer by layer, scented with jasmine.

Lorn mopped his brow and cheeks. 'I wish to God I were back in Corado,' he said in his own Ingliss-descended language, which he was gladdened to hear Ranu understood. 'This weather gets me. My clan has a lodge on the north rim of the Grann Canyon. Pines and deer and— Oh, well, it's worth a couple of years here. Not just the pay.' Briefly, something like holiness touched the heavy features. 'The work.'

'I beg your pardon,' Dhananda interrupted from the shadows, 'but no one else knows what you are telling us.'

'Oh, sorry. I forgot.' The Merican switched to his badly accented Hinji. 'I wanted to say, friends, when I finish here I'd like to go home via N'Zealann. It must be about the most interesting place on Earth. Wellantoa's damn near the capital of the planet, or will be one day, eh?'

'Perhaps!' Dhananda snapped.

'No offense,' said Lorn. 'I don't belong to the Sea People either, you know. But they are the most progressive country going.'

'In certain ways,' Dhananda conceded. 'In others—forgive me, guests, if I call your policies a little antiprogressive. For example, your consistent discouragement of attempts to civilize the world's barbarian societies.'

'Not that exactly,' defended Ranu. 'When they offer a clear threat to their neighbors, of course the Federation is among the first powers to send in the peace enforcers—which, in the long run, means psychodynamic teams, to redirect the energies of the barbarians concerned. A large-scale effort is being mounted at this moment in Sina, as I'm sure you have heard.'

'Just like you did with my ancestors, eh?' said Lorn, unabashed.

'Well, yes. But the point is, we don't want to mold anyone else into our own image; nor see them molded into the image of, say, Beneghali factory workers or Meycan peons or Orgonian foresters. So our government does exert pressure on other civilized governments to leave the institutions of backward peoples as much alone as possible.'

'Why?' Dhananda leaned forward. His beard jutted aggressively. 'It's easy enough for you Maurai. Your population growth is under control. You have your sea ranches, your synthetics plants, your worldwide commerce. Do you think the rest of mankind is better off in poverty, slavery, and ignorance?'

'Of course not,' said Alisabeta. 'But they'll get over that by themselves, in their own ways. Our trade and our example—I mean all the more advanced countries—such things can help. But they mustn't help too much, or the same thing will happen again that happened before the War of Judgment. I mean . . . what's the Hinji word? We call it cultural pseudomorphosis.'

'A mightly long word for a lady as cute as you,' said Lorn sunna Browen. He sipped his gin noisily, leaned over and patted her knee. Ranu gathered that his family had stayed behind when the Brahmards hired him for this job; and in their primness they had not furnished him with a surrogate.

'You know,' the Merican went on, 'I'm surprised that merchant seamen can talk as academically as you do.'

'Not one,' grinned Keanua, 'I'm strictly a deckhand type.'

'I notice you have a bamboo flute tucked in your sarong,' Lorn pointed out.

'Well, uh, I do play a little. To while away the watches.'

'Indeed,' murmured Dhananda. 'And your conversation is very well informed, Captain Makintairu.'

'Why shouldn't it be?' answered the Maurai, surprised. He thought of the irony if they should suspect he was not really a tramp-ship skipper. Because he was nothing else; he had been nothing else his whole adult life. 'I went to school,' he said. 'We take books along on our voyages. We talk with people in foreign ports. That's all.'

'Nevertheless—' Dhananda paused. 'It is true,' he admitted reflectively, 'that Federation citizens in general have the reputation of being rather intellectual. More, even, than would be accounted for by your admirable hundred-percent literacy rate.'

'Oh no.' Alisabeta laughed. 'I assure you, we're the least scholarly race alive. We like to learn, of course, and think and argue. But isn't that simply one of the pleasures in life, among many others? Our technology does give us abundant leisure for that sort of thing.'

'Ours doesn't,' said Dhananda grimly.

'Too many people, too few resorces,' Lorn agreed. 'You must've been to Calcut before, m'lady. But have you ever seen the slums? And I'll bet you never traveled through the hinterland and watched those poor dusty devils trying to scratch a living from the agrocollectives.'

'I did once,' said Keanua with compassion.

'Well!' Lorn shook himself, tossed off his drink, and rose. 'We've gotten far too serious. I assure you, m'lady, we aren't dry types at Corado University either. I'd like to take you and a couple of crossbows with me into the Rockies after mountain goat. . . . Come, I hear the dinner gong.' He took Alisabeta's arm.

Ranu trailed after. *Mustn't overeat,* he thought. *This night looks like the best time to start prowling.*

3

There was no moon. The time for the *Aorangi* had been chosen with that in mind. Ranu woke at midnight, as he had told himself to do. He had the common Maurai knack of sleeping a short time and being refreshed thereby. Sliding off the bed, he stood for minutes looking out and listening. The airstrip reached bare beyond the house, gray under the stars. The windows in one hangar showed light.

A sentry tramped past. His forest-green turban and

clothes, his dark face, made him another blackness. But a sheen went along his gun barrel. An actual explosive-cartridge rifle. And . . . his beat took him by this house.

Still, he was only one man. He should have been given partners. The Brahmards were as unskilled in secrecy and espionage as the Maurai. When Earth held a mere four or five scientifically-minded nations, with scant and slow traffic between them, serious conflict rarely arose. Even today Beneghal did not maintain a large army. Larger than the Federation's—but Beneghal was a land power and needed protection against barbarians. The Maurai had a near monopoly on naval strength, for a corresponding reason; and it wasn't much of a navy.

Call them, with truth, as horrible as you liked, those centuries during which the human race struggled back from the aftermath of nuclear war had had an innocence that the generations before the Judgment lacked. *I am afraid,* thought Ranu with a sadness that surprised him a bit, *we too are about to lose that particular virginity.*

No time for sentiment. '*Keanua, Alisabeta,*' he called in his head. He felt them come to alertness. '*I'm going out for a look.*'

'*Is that wise?*' The girl's worry fluttered in him. '*If you should be caught—*'

'*My chances are best now. We have them off-balance, arriving so unexpectedly. But I bet Dhananda will double his precautions tomorrow, after he's worried overnight that we may be spies.*'

'*Be careful, then,*' Keanua said. Ranu felt a kinesthetic overtone, as if a hand reached under the pillow for a knife. '*Yell if you run into trouble. I think we might fight our way clear.*'

'*Oh! Stay away from the front entrance,*' Alisabeta warned. '*When Lorn took me out on the verandah after dinner to talk, I noticed a man squatting under the willow tree there. He may just have been an old syce catching a breath of air, but more likely he's an extra watchman.*'

'*Thanks.*' Ranu omitted any flowery Maurai leave-

140

taking. His friends would be in contact. But he felt their feelings like a handclasp about him. Neither had questioned that he must be the one who ventured forth. As captain, he had the honor and obligation to assume extra hazards. Yet Keanua grumbled and fretted, and there was something in the girl's mind, less a statement than a color: she felt closer to him than to any other man.

Briefly, he wished for the physical touch of her. But—

The guard was safely past. Ranu glided out the open window.

For a space he lay flat on the verandah. Faint stirrings and voices came to him from the occupied hangar. Candles had been lit in one bungalow. The rest slept, ghostly under the sky. So far nothing was happening in the open. Ranu slithered down into the flowerbed. Too late he discovered it included roses. He bit back a sailor's oath and crouched for minutes more.

All right, better get started. He had no special training in sneakery, but most Maurai learned judo arts in school, and afterward their work and their sports kept them supple. He went like a shadow among shadows, rounding the field until he came to one of the new storehouses.

Covered by the gloom at a small rear door, he drew his knife. A great deal of miniaturized circuitry had been packed into its handle, together with a tiny accumulator cell. The jewel on the pommel was a lens, and when he touched it in the right way a pencil beam of blue light sprang forth. He examined the lock. Not plastic, nor even aluminum bronze: steel. And the door was iron reinforced. What was so valuable inside?

From Ranu's viewpoint, a ferrous lock was a lucky break. He turned the knife's inconspicuous controls, probing and grasping with magnetic pulses, resolutely suppressing the notion that every star was staring at him. After a long and sweaty while, he heard tumblers click. He opened the door gently and went through.

His beam flickered about. The interior held mostly shelves, from floor to ceiling, loaded with paperboard cartons. He padded across the room, chose a box on a rear shelf that wouldn't likely be noticed for weeks, and slit the tape. Hm . . . as expected. A dielectric energy accumulator, molecular-distortion type. Standard equipment, employed by half the powered engines in the world.

But so many—in this outpost of loneliness?

His sample was fresh, too. Uncharged. Maurai agents had already seen, from commercial aircraft that 'happened' to be blown off course, that there was only one solar-energy collection station on the whole archipelago. Nor did the islands have hydroelectric or tidal generators. Yet obviously these cells had been shipped here to be charged.

Which meant that the thing in the hills had developed much further than Federation Intelligence knew.

'Nan damn it,' Ranu whispered. 'Shark-toothed Nan damn and devour it.'

He stood for a little turning the black cube over and over in his hands. His skin prickled. Then, with a shiver, he repacked the cell and left the storehouse as quietly as he had entered.

Outside he paused. Ought he to do anything else? This one bit of information justified the whole *Aorangi* enterprise. If he tried for more and failed, and his coworkers died with him, the effort would have gone for nothing.

However. . . . Time was hideously short. An alarmed Dhananda would find ways to keep other foreigners off the island—a faked wreck or something to make the harbor unusable—until too late. At least, Ranu must assume so.

He did not agonize over his decision; that was not a Maurai habit. He made it. *Let's have a peek in that lighted hangar, just for luck, before going to bed. Tomorrow I'll try and think of some way to get inland and see the laboratory.*

A cautious half hour later, he stood flattened against a wall and peered through a window. The vaulted interior of the hangar was nearly filled by a pumped-up gasbag. Motors idled, hardly audible, propellers not yet engaged. Several mechanics were making final checks. Two men from the bungalow where candles had been lit—

Brahmards themselves, to judge from their white garb and authoritative manner—stood waiting while some junior attendants loaded boxed apparatus into the gondola. Above the whirr, Ranu caught a snatch of talk between them:

'—unsanctified hour. Why *now,* for Vishnu's sake?'

'Those fool newcomers. They might not be distressed mariners, ever think of that? In any case, they mustn't see us handling stuff like this.' Four men staggered past bearing a coiled cable. The uninsulated ends shone the red of pure copper. 'You don't use that for geographical research, what?'

Renau felt his hair stir.

Two soldiers embarked with guns. Ranu doubted they were going along merely because of the monetary value of that cable, fabulous though it was.

The scientists followed. The ground crew manned a capstan. Their ancient, wailing chant came like a protest—that human muscles must so strain when a hundred horses snored in the same room. The hangar roof and front wall folded creakily aside.

Ranu went rigid.

He must unconsciously have shot his thought to the other Maurai. *'No!'* Alisabeta cried to him.

Keanua said more slowly: *'That's cannibal recklessness, skipper. You might fall and smear yourself over three degrees of latitude. Or if you should be seen—'* ..

'I'll never have a better chance,' Ranu said. *'We've already invented a dozen different cover stories in case I disappear. So pick one and use it.'*

'But you,' Alisabeta begged. *'Alone out there!'*

'It might be worse for you, if Dhananda should decide to get tough,' Ranu answered. The Ingliss singlemindedness had come upon him, overriding the easy, indolent Maurai blood. But then that second heritage woke with a shout, for those who first possessed N'Zealann, the canoe men and moa hunters, would have dived laughing into an escapade like this.

He pushed down the glee and related what he had found in the storehouse. *'If you feel any doubt about your own safety, any time, forget me and leave,'* he ordered. *'Intelligence has got to know at least this much. If I'm detected yonder in the hills, I'll try to get away and hide in the jungle.'* The hangar was open, the aircraft slipping its cables, the propellers becoming bright transparent circles as they were engaged. *'Farewell. Good luck.'*

'Tanaroa be with you,' Alisabeta called through her tears.

Ranu dashed around the corner. The aircraft rose on a slant, gondola an ebony slab, bag a pale storm cloud. The propellers threw wind in his face. He ran along the vessel's shadow, poised, and sprang.

Almost, he didn't make it. His fingers closed on something, slipped, clamped with the strength of terror. Both hands, now! He was gripping an ironwood bar, part of the mooring gear, his legs adangle over an earth that fell away below him with appalling swiftness. He sucked in a breath and chinned himself, got one knee over the bar, clung there and gasped.

The electric motors purred. A breeze whittered among struts and spars. Otherwise Ranu was alone with his heartbeat. After a while it slowed. He hitched himself to a slightly more comfortable crouch and looked about. The jungle was black, dappled with dark gray, far underneath him. The sea that edged it shimmered in starlight with exactly the same whiteness as the nacelles along the gondola. He heard a friendly creaking of wickerwork, felt a sort of throb as the gasbag expanded in this higher-level air. The constellations wheeled grandly around him.

He had read about jet aircraft that outpaced the sun, before the nuclear war. Once he had seen a representation, on a fragment of ancient cinema film discovered by archeologists and transferred to new acetate; a sound track had been included. He did not understand how anyone could want to sit locked in a howling coffin like that when he might have swum through the air, intimate with the night sky, as Ranu was now doing.

However precariously, his mind added with wryness.

He had not been seen, and he probably wasn't affecting the trim enough to make the pilot suspicious. Nevertheless, he had scant time to admire the view. The bar along which he sprawled, the sisal guy on which he leaned one shoulder, dug into his flesh. His muscles were already tiring. If this trip was any slower than he had guessed it would be, he'd tumble to earth.

Or else be too clumsy to spring off unseen and melt into darkness as the aircraft landed.

Or when he turned up missing in the morning, Dhananda might guess the truth and lay a trap for him.

Or anything! Stop your fuss, you idiot. You need all your energy for hanging on.

4

The Brahmard's tread was light on the verandah, but Alisabeta's nerves were strung so taut that she sensed him and turned about with a small gasp. For a second they regarded each other, unspeaking, the dark, slight, bearded man in his neat whites and the strongly built girl whose skin seemed to glow golden in the shade of a trellised grapevine. Beyond, the airstrip flimmered in midmorning sunlight. Heat hazes wavered on the hangar roofs.

'You have not found him?' she asked at last, without tone.

Dhananda's head shook slowly, as if his turban had become heavy. 'No. Not a trace. I came back to ask you if you have any idea where he might have gone.'

'I told your deputy my guess. Ranu . . . Captain Makintairu is in the habit of taking a swim before breakfast. He may have gone down to the shore about dawn and—' She hoped he would take her hesitation to mean no more than an unspoken: *Sharks. Rip tides. Cramp.*

But the sable gaze continued to probe her. 'It is most improbable that he could have left this area unobserved,' Dhananda said. 'You have seen our guards. More of them are posted downhill.'

'What are you guarding against?' she counterattacked,

to divert him. 'Are you less popular with the natives than you claim to be?'

He parried her almost contemptuously: 'We have reason to think two of the Buruman pirate kings have made alliance and gotten some aircraft. We do have equipment and materials here that would be worth stealing. Now, about Captain Makintairu. I cannot believe he left unseen unless he did so deliberately, taking great trouble about it. Why?'

'I don't know I tell you!'

'You must admit we are duty bound to consider the possibility that you are not simple merchant mariners.'

'What else? Pirates ourselves? Don't be absurd.' *I dare you to accuse us of being spies. Because then I will ask what there is here to spy on.*

Only . . . then what will you do?

Dhananda struck the porch railing with a fist. Bitterness spoke: 'Your Federation swears so piously it doesn't intervene in the development of other cultures.'

'Except when self-defense forces us to,' Alisabeta said. 'And only a minimum.'

He ignored that. 'In the name of nonintervention, you are always prepared to refuse some country the searanching equipment that would give it a new start, or bribe somebody else *with* such equipment not to begin a full-fledged merchant service to a third and backward country . . . a service that might bring the backward country up-to-date in less than a generation. You talk about encouraging cultural diversity. You seem seriously to believe it's moral keeping the Okkaidans impoverished fishermen so they'll be satisfied to write haiku and grow dwarf gardens for recreation. And yet—by Kali herself, your agents are everywhere!'

'If you don't want us here,' Alisabeta snapped, 'deport us and complain to our government.'

'I may have to do more than that.'

'But I swear—'

'Alisabeta! Keanua!'

Distance-attenuated, Ranu's message still stiffened her where she stood. She felt his tension, and an undertone

146

of hunger and thirst, like a thrum along her own nerves. The verandah faded about her, and she stood in murk and heard a slamming of great pumps. Was there really a red warning light that went flash-flash-flash above a bank of transformers taller than a man?

'Yes, I'm inside,' the rapid blurred voice said in her skull. 'I watched my chance from the jungle edge. When an oxcart came along the trail with a sleepy native driver, I clung to the bottom and was carried through the gates. Food supplies. Evidently the workers here have a contract with some nearby village. The savages bring food and do guard duty. I've seen at least three of them prowling about with blowguns. Anyhow, I'm in. I dropped from the cart and slipped into a side tunnel. Now I'm sneaking around, hoping not to be seen.

'The place is huge! They must have spent years enlarging a chain of natural caves. Air conduits everywhere—I daresay that's how our signals are getting through; I sense you, but faintly. Forced ventilation, with thermostatic controls. Can you imagine power expenditure on such a scale? I'm going toward the center of things now for a look. My signal will probably be screened out till I come back near the entrance again.'

'Don't, skipper,' Keanua pleaded. 'You've seen plenty. We know for a fact that Intelligence guessed right. That's enough.'

'Not quite,' Ranu said. The Maurai rashness flickered along the edge of his words. 'I want to see if the project is as far advanced as I fear. If not, perhaps the Federation won't have to take emergency measures. I'm afraid we will, though.'

'Ranu!' Alisabeta called. His thought enfolded her. But static exploded, interfering energies that hurt her perceptions. When it lifted, an emptiness was in her head where Ranu had been.

'Are you ill, my lady?' Dhananda barked the question.

She looked dazedly out at the sky, unable to answer. He moved nearer. 'What are you doing?' he pressed.

'Steady girl,' Keanua rumbled.

Alisabeta swallowed, squared her shoulders and faced

147

the Brahmard. 'I'm worrying about Captain Makintairu,' she said coldly. 'Does that satisfy you?'

'No.'

'Hoy, there, you!' rang a voice from the front door. Lorn sunna Browen came forth. His kilted form over-topped them both; the light eyes sparked at Dhananda. 'What kind of hospitality is this? Is he bothering you, my lady?'

'I am not certain that these people have met the obligations of guests,' Dhananda said, his control cracking open.

Lorn put arms akimbo, fists knotted. 'Until you can prove that, though, just watch your manners. Eh? As long as I'm here, this is my house, not yours.'

'Please,' Alisabeta said. She hated fights. Why had she ever volunteered for this job? 'I beg you . . . don't.'

Dhananda made a jerky bow. 'Perhaps I am overzealous,' he said without conviction. 'If so, I ask your pardon. I shall continue the search for the captain.'

'I think—meanwhile—I'll go down to our ship and help Keanua with the repairs,' Alisabeta whispered.

'Very well,' said Dhananda.

Lorn took her arm. 'Mind if I come too? You, uh, you might like to have a little distraction from thinking about your poor friend. And I never have seen an oceangoing craft close by. They flew me here when I was hired.'

'I suggest you return to your own work, sir,' Dhananda said in a harsh tone.

'When I'm good and ready, I will,' Lorn answered airily. 'Come, Miss . . . uh . . . m' lady.' He led Alisabeta down the stair and around the strip. Dhananda watched from the portico, motionless.

'You mustn't mind him,' Lorn said after a bit. 'He's not a bad sort. A nice family man, in fact, pretty good chess player, and a devil on the polo field. But this has been a long grind, and his responsibility has kind of worn him down.'

'Oh yes. I understand,' Alisabeta said. *But still he frightens me.*

Lorn ran a hand through his thinning yellow mane.

'Most Brahmards are pretty decent,' he said. 'I've come to know them in the time I've been working here. They're recruited young, you know, with psychological tests to weed out those who don't have the . . . the dedication, I guess you'd call it. Oh, sure, naturally they enjoy being a boss caste. But somebody has to be. No Hinjan country has the resources or the elbow room to govern itself as loosely as you Sea People do. The Brahmards want to modernize Beneghal—eventually the world. Get mankind back where it was before the War of Judgment, and go on from there.'

'I know,' Alisabeta said.

'I don't see why you Maurai are so dead set against that. Don't you realize how many people go to bed hungry every night?'

'Of course, of course we do!' she burst out. It angered her that tears should come so close to the surface of her eyes. 'But so they did before the War. Can't anyone else see . . . turning the planet into one huge factory isn't the answer? Have you read any history? Did you ever hear of . . . oh, just to name one movement that called itself progressive . . . the Communists? They too were going to end poverty and famine. They were going to reorganize society along rational lines. Well, we have contemporary records to prove that in Rossaya alone, in the first thirty or forty years it had power, their regime killed twenty million of their own citizens. Starved them, shot them, worked them to death in labor camps. The total deaths, in all the Communist countries, may have gone as high as a hundred million. And this was *before* evangelistic foreign policies brought on nuclear war. How many famines and plagues would it take to wipe out that many human lives? And how much was the life of the survivors worth, under such masters?'

'But the Brahmards aren't like that,' he protested. 'See for yourself, down in this village. The natives are well taken care of. Nobody abuses them or coerces them. Same thing on the mainland. There's a lot of misery yet in Beneghal—mass starvation going on right now—but it'll be overcome.'

'Why haven't the villagers been fishing?' she challenged.

'Eh?' Taken aback, Lorn paused on the downhill path. The sun poured white across them both, made the bay a bowl of molten brass, and seemed to flatten the jungle leafage into one solid listless green. The air was very empty and quiet. But Ranu crept through the belly of a mountain, where machines hammered. . . .

'Well, it hasn't been practical to allow that,' said the Merican. 'Some of our work is confidential. We can't risk information leaking out. But the Beneghalis have been feeding them. Oktai, it amounts to a holiday for the fishers. They aren't complaining.'

Alisabeta decided to change the subject, or even this big bundle of guilelessness might grow suspicious. 'So you're a scientist,' she said. 'How interesting. But what do they need you here for? I mean, they have good scientists of their own.'

'I . . . uh . . . I have specialized knowledge which is, uh, applicable,' he said. 'You know how the sciences and technologies hang together. Your Island biotechs breed new species to concentrate particular metals out of seawater, so naturally they need metallurgic data too. In my own case—uh—' Hastily: 'I do want to visit your big observatory in N'Zealann on my way home. I hear they've photographed an ancient artificial satellite, still circling the Earth after all these centuries. I think maybe some of the records our archeologists have dug up in Merica would enable us to identify it. Knowing its original orbit and so forth, we could compute out a lot of information about the solar system.'

'Tanaroa, yes!' Despite everything, eagerness jumped in her.

His red face, gleaming with sweat, lifted toward the blank blue sky. 'Of course,' he murmured, almost to himself, 'that's a piddle compared to what we'd learn if we could get back out there in person.'

'Build space probes again? Or actual manned ships?'

'Yes. If we had the power, and the industrial plant. By Oktai, but I get sick of this!' Lorn exclaimed. His grip on her arm tightened unconsciously until she winced. 'Scraping along on lean ores, tailings, scrap, synthetics, substitutes . . . because the ancients exhausted so much. Exhausted the good mines, most of the fossil fuels, coal, petroleum, uranium . . . then smashed their industry in the War and let the machines corrode away to unrecoverable dust in the dark ages that followed. That's what's holding us back, girl. We know everything our ancestors did and then some. But we haven't got the equipment they had to process materials on the scale they did, and we haven't the natural resources to rebuild that equipment. A vicious circle. We haven't got the capital to make it economically feasible to produce the giant industries that could accumulate the capital.'

'I think we're doing quite well,' she said, gently disengaging herself. 'Sunpower, fuel cells, wind and water, biotechnology, sea ranches and sea farms, efficient agriculture—'

'We could do better, though.' His arm swept a violent arc that ended with a finger pointed at the bay. 'There! The oceans. Every element in the periodic table is dissolved in them. Billions of tons. But we'll never get more than a minimum out with your fool solar and biological methods. We need energy. Power to evaporate water by the cubic kilometer. Power to synthesize oil by the megabarrel. Power to go to the stars.'

The rapture faded. He seemed shaken by his own words, shut his lips as if retreating behind the walrus moustache, and resumed walking. Alisabeta came along in silence. Their feet scrunched in gravel and sent up little puffs of dust. Presently the dock resounded under them; they boarded the *Aorangi*, and went across to the engine-room hatch.

Keanua paused in his labors as they entered. He had opened the aluminum-alloy casing and spread parts out on the deck, where he squatted in a sunbeam from an open porthole. Elsewhere the room was cool and shadowy; wavelets lapped the hull.

'Good day,' said the Taiitian. His smile was perfunctory, his thoughts inside the mountain with Ranu.

151

'Looks as if you're immobilized for a while,' Lorn said, lounging back against a flame-grained bulkhead panel.

'Until we find what has happened to our friend, surely,' Keanua answered.

'I'm sorry about him,' Lorn said. 'I hope he comes back soon.'

'Well, we can't wait indefinitely for him,' Alisabeta made herself say. 'If he isn't found by the time the engine is fixed, best we start for Calcut. Your group will send him on when he does appear, won't you?'

'Sure,' said Lorn. 'If he's alive. Uh, 'scuse me, my lady.'

'No offense. We don't hold with euphemisms in the Islands.'

'It does puzzle the deuce out of me,' Keanua grunted. 'He's a good swimmer, if he did go for a swim. Of course, he might have taken a walk instead, into the jungle. Are you sure the native tribes are always peaceful?'

'Um—'

'Can you hear me? Can you hear me?'

Ranu's voice was as tiny in Alisabeta's head as the scream of an insect. But they felt the pain that jagged in it. He had been wounded.

'Get out! Get away as fast as you can! I've seen—the thing—it's working! I swear it must be working. Pouring out power . . . some kind of chemosynthetic plan beyond—They saw me as I started back. Put a blowgun dart in my thigh. Alarms hooting everywhere. I think I can beat them to the entrance, though, get into the forest—'

Keanua had leaped to his feet. The muscles moved like snakes under his skin. *'Escape, with natives tracking you?'* he snarled.

Ranu's signal strengthened as he came nearer the open air. *'This place has radiophone contact with the town. Dhananda's undoubtedly being notified right now. Get clear, you two!'*

'If . . . if we can,' Alisabeta faltered. 'But you—'

'GET UNDER WEIGH, I TELL YOU!'

5

Lorn stared from one to another of them. 'What's wrong?' A hand dropped to his knife. Years at a desk had not much slowed his mountaineer's reflexes.

Alisabeta glanced past him at Keanua. There was no need for words. The Taiitian's grasp closed on Lorn's dagger wrist.

'What the hell—!' The Merican yanked with skill. His arm snapped out between the thumb and fingers holding him, and a sunbeam flared off steel.

Keanua closed in. His left arm batted sideways to deflect the knife. His right hand, stiffly held, poked at the solar plexus. But Lorn's left palm came chopping down, edge on. A less burly wrist than Keanua's would have broken. As it was, the sailor choked on an oath and went pale around the nostrils. Lorn snatched his opponent's knife from the sheath and threw it out the porthole.

The Merican could then have ripped Keanua's belly. But instead he paused. 'What's got into you?' he asked in a high, bewildered voice. 'Miss Alisa—' He half looked around for her.

Keanua recovered enough to go after the clansman's dagger. One arm under the wrist for a fulcrum, the other arm applying the leverage of his whole body—Lorn's hand bent down, the fingers were pulled open by their own tendons, the blade tinkled to the deck. 'Get it, girl!' Keanua said. He kicked it aside. Lorn had already grappled him.

Alisabeta slipped past their trampling legs to snatch the weapon. Her pulse thuttered in her throat. It was infinitely horrible that the sun should pour so brilliant through the porthole. The chuckle of water on the hull was lost in the rough breath and stamp of feet, back and forth as the fight swayed. Lorn struck with a poleax fist, but Keanua dropped his head and took the blow on his skull. Anguish stabbed through the Merican's knuckles. He let go his adversary. Keanua followed the advantage, seeking a stranglehold. Lorn's foot lashed out, caught the Taiitian in the stomach, sent him lurching away.

No time to gape! Alisabeta ran up the ladder onto the main deck. A few black children stood on the wharf, sucking their thumbs and staring endlessly at the ship. Except for them, Port Arberta seemed asleep. But no, yonder in the heat shimmer . . . dust on the downhill path. . . . She shaded her eyes. A man in white and three soldiers in green; headed this way, surely. Dhananda had been informed that a spy had entered the secret place. Now he was on his way to arrest the spy's indubitable accomplices.

But with only three men?

Wait! He doesn't know about head-to-head. He can't tell that we here know he knows about Ranu. So he plans to capture us by surprise—so we won't destroy evidence or scuttle the ship or something—Yes, he'll come aboard with some story about searching for Ranu, and have his men aim their guns at us when he makes a signal. Not before.

'Ranu, what should I do?'

There was no answer, only—when she concentrated—a sense of pain in the muscles, fire in the lungs, heat and sweat and running. He fled through the jungle with the blowgun men on his trail, unable to think of anything but a hiding place.

Alisabeta bit her nails. Lesu Haristi, Son of Tanaroa, what to do, what to do? She had been about to call the advance base on Car Nicbar. A single radio shout, to tell them what had been learned, and then surrender to Dhananda. But that was a desperation measure. It would openly involve the Federation government. Worse, any outsider who happened to be tuned to that band—and considerable radio talk went on these days—might well record and decode and get some inkling of what was here and tell the world. And this would in time start similar kettles boiling elsewhere . . . and the Federation couldn't sit on that many lids, didn't want to, wasn't

154

equipped to—*Stop maundering, you ninny! Make up your mind!*

Alisabeta darted back down into the engine room. Keanua and Lorn rolled on the deck, locked together. She picked a wrench from among the tools and poised it above the Merican's head. His scalp shone pinkly through the yellow hair, a bald spot, and last night he had shown her pictures of his children. . . . No. She couldn't. She threw the wrench aside, pulled off her lap-lap, folded it into a strip, and drew it carefully around Lorn's throat. A twist; he choked and released Keanua; the Taiitian got a grip and throttled him unconscious in thirty seconds.

'Thanks! Don't know . . . if I could have done that . . . alone. Strong's an orca, him.' As he talked Keanua deftly bound and gagged the Merican. Lorn stirred, blinked, writhed helplessly, and glared his hurt and anger.

Alisabeta had already slid back a certain panel. The compartment behind held the other engine, the one that was not damaged. She connected it to the gears while she told Keanua what she had seen. 'If we work it right, I think we can also capture those other men,' she said. 'That'll cause confusion, and they'll be useful hostages, am I right?'

'Right. Good girl.' Keanua slapped her bottom and grinned. Remembering Beneghali customs, she put the lap-lap on again and went topside.

Dhananda and his guards reached the dock a few minutes later. She waved at them but kept her place by the saloon cabin door. They crossed the gangplank, which boomed under their boots. The Brahmard's countenance was stormy. 'Where are the others?' he demanded.

'In there.' She nodded at the cabin. 'Having a drink. Won't you join us?'

He hesitated. 'If you will too, my lady.'

'Of course.' She went ahead. The room was long, low, and cool, furnished with little more than straw mats and shoji screens. Keanua stepped from behind one of them. He held a repeating blowgun.

155

'Stay where you are, friends,' he ordered around the mouthpiece. 'Raise your hands.'

A soldier spat a curse and snatched for his submachine gun. Keanua puffed. The feeder mechanism clicked. Three darts buried themselves in the planking at the soldier's feet. 'Cyanide,' Keanua reminded them. He kept the bamboo tube steady. 'Next time I aim to kill.'

'What do you think you are doing?' Dhananda breathed. His features had turned almost gray. But he lifted his arms with the others. Alisabeta took their weapons. She cast the guns into a corner as if they were hot to the touch.

'Secure them,' Keanua said. He made the prisoners lie down while the girl hogtied them. Afterward he carried each below through a hatch in the saloon deck to a locker where Lorn already lay. As he made Dhananda fast to a shackle bolt he said, 'We're going to make a break for it. Would you like to tell your men ashore to let us go without a fight? I'll run a microphone down here for you.'

'No,' Dhananda said. 'You pirate swine.'

'Suit yourself. But if we get sunk you'll drown too. Think about that.' Keanua went back topside.

Alisabeta stood by the cabin door, straining into a silence that hissed. 'I can't hear him at all,' she said from the verge of tears. 'Is he dead?'

'No time for that now,' Keanua said. 'We've got to get started. Take the wheel. I think once we're past the headland, we'll pick up a little wind.'

She nodded dumbly and went to the pilothouse. Keanua cast off. Several adult villagers materialized as if by sorcery to watch. The engine pulsed, screws caught the water, the *Aorangi* stood out into the bay. Keanua moved briskly about, preparing the ship's armament. It was standard for a civilian vessel: a catapult throwing bombs of jellied fish oil, two flywheel guns that cast streams of small sharp rocks. Since pirates couldn't get gunpowder, merchantmen saw no reason to pay its staggering cost. One of the Intelligence officers had wanted to supply a rocket launcher, but Ranu had pointed out that it would be hard enough to conceal the extra engine.

Men must be swarming like ants on the hilltop. Alisabeta watched four of them come down on horseback. The dust smoked behind them. They flung open the doors of a boathouse and emerged in a watercraft that zoomed within hailing distance.

A Beneghali officer rose in the stern sheets and bawled through a megaphone—his voice was soon lost on that sun-dazzled expanse—'Ahoy, there! Where are you bound?'

'Your chief's commandeered us to make a search,' Keanua shouted back.

'Yes? Where is he? Let me speak to him.'

'He's below. Can't come now.'

'Stand by to be boarded.'

Keanua said rude things. Alisabeta guided the ship out through the channel, scarcely hearing. Partly she was fighting down a sense of sadness and defilement—she had attacked guests—and partly she kept crying for Ranu to answer. Only the gulls did.

The boat darted back to shore. Keanua came aft. 'They'll be at us before long,' he said bleakly. 'I told 'em their own folk would go down with us, and they'd better negotiate instead. Implying we really are pirates, you know. But they wouldn't listen.'

'Certainly not,' Alisabeta said. 'Every hour of haggling is time gained for us. They know that.'

Keanua sighed. 'Well, so it goes. I'll holler to Nicbar.'

'What signal?' Though cipher messages would be too risky, a few codes had been agreed upon: mere standardized impulses, covering preset situations.

'Attack. Come here as fast as they can with everything they've got,' Keanua decided.

'Just to save our lives? Oh no!'

The Taiitian shook his head. 'To wipe out that damned project in the hills. Else the Brahmards will get the idea, and mount so big a guard from now on that we won't be able to come near without a full-scale war.'

He stood quiet awhile. 'Two of us on this ship, and a

couple hundred of them,' he said. 'We'll have a tough time staying alive, girl, till the relief expedition gets close enough for a head-to-head.' He yawned and stretched, trying to ease his tension. 'Of course, I'd rather like to stay alive for my own sake, too.'

There was indeed a breeze on the open sea, which freshened slightly as the *Aorangi* moved south. They set the computer to direct sail hoisting and disengaged the screws. The engine would be required at full capacity to power the weapons. After putting the wheel on autopilot, Keanua and Alisabeta helped each other into quilted combat armor and alloy helmets.

Presently the airships came aloft. That was the sole possible form of onslaught, she knew. With their inland mentalities, the Brahmards had stationed no naval units here. There were—one, two, three—a full dozen vessels, big and bright in the sky. They assumed formation and lined out in pursuit.

6

Ranu awoke so fast that for a moment he blinked about him in wonderment: where was he, what had happened? He lay in a hollow beneath a fallen tree, hidden by a cascade of trumpet-flower vines. The sun turned their leaves nearly yellow; the light here behind them was thick and green, the air unspeakably hot. He couldn't be sure how much of the crawling over his body was sweat and how much was ants. His right thigh needled him where the dart had pierced it. A smell of earth and crushed vegetation filled his nostrils, mingled with his own stench. Nothing but his heartbeat and the distant liquid notes of a bulbul interrupted noonday silence.

Oh yes, he recalled wearily. *I got out the main entrance. Stiff-armed a sentry and sprang into the brush. A score of Beneghalis after me . . . shook them, but just plain had to outrun the natives . . . longer legs. I hope I covered my trail, once beyond their sight. Must have, or they'd've found me here by now. I've been unconscious for hours.*

The ship!

Remembrance rammed into him. He sucked a breath between his teeth, nearly jumped from his hiding place, recovered his wits and dug fingers into the mold under his belly. At last he felt able to reach forth head-to-head.

'*Alisabeta! Are you there? Can you hear me?*'

Her answer was instant. Not words—a gasp, a laugh, a sob, clearer and stronger than he had ever known before; and as their minds embraced, some deeper aspect of self. Suddenly he became her, aboard the ship.

No more land was to be seen, only the ocean, blue close at hand, shining like mica farther out where the sun smote it. The wreckage of an aircraft bobbed a kilometer to starboard, gondola projecting from beneath the flattened bag. The other vessels maneuvered majestically overhead. Their propeller whirr drifted across an empty deck.

The *Aorangi* had taken a beating. Incendiaries could not ignite fireproofed material, but had left scorches everywhere. The cabins were kindling wood. A direct hit with an explosive bomb had shattered the foremast, which lay in a tangle across the smashed sun-power collectors. The after boom trailed overside. What sails were still on the yards hung in rags. A near miss had opened two compartments in the port hull, so that the trimaran was low on that side, the deck crazily tilted.

Three dead men sprawled amidships in a black spatter of clotting blood. Ranu recollected with Alisabeta's horror: when an aircraft sank grapnels into the fore-skysail and soldiers came swarming down ropes, she hosed them with stones. Most had dropped overboard, but those three hit with nauseating sounds. Then Keanua, at the catapult, put four separate fire-shells into the gasbag. Even against modern safety devices, that served to touch off the hydrogen. The aircraft cast loose and drifted slowly seaward. The flames were pale, nearly invisible in the light, but steam puffed high when it ditched. The

Maurai, naturally, made no attempt to hinder the rescue operation that followed. Later the Beneghalis had been content with bombing and strafing. Once the defenders were out of action, they could board with no difficulty.

'They aren't pressing the attack as hard as they might,' Keanua reported. *'But then, they hope to spare our prisoners, and don't know we have reinforcements coming. If we can hold out that long—'* He sensed how close was the rapport between Ranu and the girl, and withdrew with an embarrassed apology. Still, Ranu had had time to share the pain of burns and a pellet in his shoulder.

Alisabeta crouched in the starboard slugthrower turret. It was hot and dark and vibrated with the whining flywheel. The piece of sky in her sights was fiery blue, a tatter of sail was blinding white. He felt her fear. Too many bomb splinters, too many concussion blows, had already weakened this plywood shelter. An incendiary landing just outside would not set it afire, but could pull out the oxygen. *'So, so,'* Ranu caressed her. *'I am here now.'* Their hands swung the gun about.

The lead airship peeled off the formation and lumbered into view. For the most part the squadron had passed well above missile range and dropped bombs—using crude sights, luckily. But the last several passes had been strafing runs. Keanua thought that was because their explosives were nearly used up. The expenditure of high-energy chemicals had been great, even for an industrialized power like Beneghal. Alisabeta believed they were concerned for the prisoners.

No matter. Here they came!

The airship droned low above the gaunt A of the mainmast. Its shadow swooped before it. So did a pellet storm, rocks thunking, booming, skittering, the deck atremble under their impact. Alisabeta and Ranu got the enemy's forward gun turret, a thick wooden bulge on the gondola, in their sights. They pressed the pedal that engaged the feeder. Their weapon came to life with a howl. Stones flew against the wickerwork above.

From the catapult emplacement, Keanua roared. Alisabeta heard him this far aft. A brief and frightful clatter drowned him out. The airship fell off course, wobbled, veered, and drifted aside. The girl saw the port nacelle blackened and dented. Keanua had scored a direct hit on that engine, disabled it, crippled the flyer.

'Hurrao!' Renu whooped.

Alisabeta leaned her forehead on the gun console. She shivered with exhaustion. '*How long can we go on like this? Our magazines will soon be empty. Our sun cells are almost drained, and no way to recharge them. Don't let me faint, Ranu. Hold me, my dear—*'

'*It can't be much longer. Modern military airships can do a hundred kilometers per hour. The base on Car Nicbar isn't more than four hundred kilometers away. Any moment.*'

This moment!

Again Keanua shouted. Alisabeta dared step out on deck for a clear view, gasped, and leaned against the turret. The Beneghalis, at their altitude, had seen the menace well before now. That last assault on the *Aorangi* was made in desperation. They marshaled themselves for battle.

Still distant, but rapidly swelling, came fifteen lean golden-painted ships. Each had four spendthrift engines to drive it through the sky; each was loaded with bombs and slugs and aerial harpoons. The Beneghalis had spent their ammunition on the *Aorangi*.

As the newcomers approached, Ranu-Alisabeta made out their insignia. Not Maurai, of course; not anything, though the dragons looked rather Sinese. Rumor had long flown about a warlord in Yunnan who had accumulated sufficient force to attempt large-scale banditry. On the other hand, there were always upstart buccaneers from Buruma, Iryan, or from as far as Smalilann—

'*Get back under cover,*' Ranu warned Alisabeta. '*Anything can happen yet.*' When she was safe, he sighed. '*Now my own job starts.*'

'Ranu, no, you're hurt.'

'*They'll need a guide. Farewell for now. Tanaroa be with you ......till I come back.*'

Gently, he disengaged himself. His thought flashed upward. *'Ranu Makintairu calling. Can you hear me?'*

'Loud and clear.' Aruwera Samitu, chief Intelligence officer aboard the flagship, meshed minds and whistled. *'You've had a thin time of it, haven't you?'*

'Well, we've gotten off easier than we had any right to, considering how far the situation has progressed. Listen. Your data fitted into a picture which was perfectly correct, but three or four years obsolete. The Brahmards are not just building an atomic power station here. They've built it. It's operating.'

'What!'

'I swear it must be.' Swiftly, Ranu sketched what he had seen. *'It can't have been completed very long, or we'd be facing some real opposition. In fact, the research team is probably still busy getting a few final bugs out. But essentially the work is complete. As your service deduced, the Beneghalis didn't have the scientific resources to do this themselves, on the basis of ancient data. I'd guess they got pretty far, but couldn't quite make the apparatus go. So they imported Lorn sunna Browen. And he, with his knowledge of nuclear processes in the stars, developed a fresh approach. I can't imagine what. But . . . they've done something on this island that the whole ancient world never achieved. Controlled hydrogen fusion.'*

'Is the plant very big?'

'Tremendous. But the heart seems to be in one room. A circular chamber lined with tall iron cores. I hardly dare guess how many tons of iron. They must have combed the world.'

'They did. That was our first clue. Our own physicists think the reaction must be contained by magnetic fields—But no time for that. The air battle's beginning. I expect we can clear away these chaps within an hour. Can you, then, guide us in?'

'Yes. After I've located myself. Good luck.'

Ranu focused attention back on his immediate surroundings. Let's see, early afternoon, so that direction was west, and he'd escaped along an approximate southeasterly track. Setting his jaws against the pain in his leg, he crawled from the hollow and limped into the cane-brakes.

His progress was slow, with many pauses to climb a tree and get the lay of the land. It seemed to him that he was making enough noise to rouse Nan down in watery hell. More than an hour passed before he came on a man-made path, winding between solid walls of brush. Ruts bespoke wagons, which meant it ran from some native village to the caves. By now Ranu's chest was laboring too hard for him to exercise any forester's caution. He set off along the road.

The jungle remained hot and utterly quiet. He felt he could hear anyone else approaching in plenty of time to hide. But the Annamanese caught him unexpectedly.

They leaped from an overhead branch, two dark dwarfs in loincloths, armed with daggers and blowguns. Ranu hardly glimpsed them as they fell. He had no time to think, only to react. His left hand chopped at a skinny neck. He heard a cracking sound. The native dropped like a stone.

The other one squealed and scuttered aside. Ranu drew his knife. The blowgun rose. Ranu charged. He was dimly aware of the dart as it went past his ear. It wasn't poisoned—the Annamanese left that sort of thing to the civilized nations—but it could have reached his heart. He caught the tube and yanked it away. Fear-widened eyes bulged at him. The savage pulled out his dagger and stabbed. He was not very skillful. Ranu parried the blow, taking only a minor slash on his forearm, and drove his own blade home. The native wailed. Ranu hit again.

Then there was nothing but sunlit thick silence and two bodies that looked still smaller than when they had lived. *Merciful Lesu, did I have to do this?*

Come on, Ranu. Pick up those feet of yours. He closed the staring eyes and continued on his way. When he was near the caverns, he found a hiding place and waited.

Not for long. Such Beneghali aircraft as did not go into the sea fled. They took a stand above Port Arberta, prepared to defend it against slavers. But the Maurai left a guard at hover near the watership and cruised on past, inland over the hills. Ranu resumed contact with Aruwera, who relayed instructions to the flagship navigation officer. Presently the raiders circled above the power laboratory.

Soldiers—barbarically painted and clad—went down by parachute. The fight on the ground was bitter but short. When the last sentry had run into the woods, the Maurai swarmed through the installation.

In the cold fluorescent light that an infinitesimal fraction of its output powered, Aruwera looked upon the fusion reactor with awe. 'What a thing!' he kept breathing. 'What a *thing!*'

'I hate to destroy it,' said his chief scientific aide. 'Tanaroa! I'll have bad dreams for the rest of my life. Can't we at least salvage the plans?'

'If we can find them in time to microphotograph,' Aruwera said. 'Otherwise they'll have to be burned as part of the general vandalism. Pirates wouldn't steal blueprints. We've got to wreck everything as if for the sake of the iron and whatever else looks commercially valuable . . . load the loot and be off before the whole Beneghali air force arrives from the mainland. And, yes, send a signal to dismantle the Car Nicbar base. Let's get busy. Where's the main shutoff switch?'

The scientist began tracing circuits fast and knowingly, but with revulsion still in him. 'How much did this cost?' he wondered. 'How much of this country's wealth are we robbing?'

'Quite a bit,' said Ranu. He spat. 'I don't care about that, though. Maybe now they can tax their peasants less. What I do care about—' He broke off. Numerous Beneghalis and some Maurai had died today. The military professionals around him would not understand how the memory hurt, of two little black men lying dead in the jungle, hardly bigger than children.

7

The eighth International Physical Society convention was held in Wellantoa. It was more colorful than previous ones, for several other nations (tribes, clans, alliances, societies, religions, anarchisms . . . whatever the more or less political unit might be in a particular civilization) had now developed to the point of supporting physicists. Robes, drawers, breastplates, togas joined the accustomed sarongs and tunics and kilts. At night, music on a dozen different scales wavered from upper-level windows. Those who belonged to poetically minded cultures struggled to translate each other's compositions, and often took the basic idea into their own repertory. On the professional side, there were a number of outstanding presentations, notably a Maurai computer that used artificial organic tissue and a Brasilean mathematician's generalized theory of turbulence processes.

Lorn sunna Browen was a conspicuous attender. Not that many people asked him about his Thrilling Adventure with the Pirates. That had been years ago, after all, and he'd given short answers from the first. 'They kept us on some desert island till the ransom came, then they set us off near Port Arberta after dark. We weren't mistreated. Mainly we were bored.' Lorn's work on stellar evolution was more interesting.

However, the big balding man disappeared several times from the convention lodge. He spoke to odd characters down on the waterfront; money went from hand to hand; at last he got a message that brought a curiously grim chuckle from him. Promptly he went into the street and hailed a pedicab.

He got out at a house in the hills above the city. A superb view of groves and gardens sloped down to the harbor, thronged with masts under the afternoon sun. Even in their largest town, the Sea People didn't like to be crowded. This dwelling was typical: whitewashed brick, red tile roof, riotous flowerbeds. A pennant on the flagpole, under the Cross and Stars, showed that a ship-master lived here.

When he was home. But the hired prowler had said Captain Makintairu was currently at sea. His wife had stayed ashore this trip, having two children in school and a third soon to be born. The Merican dismissed the cab and strode over the path to the door. He knocked.

The door opened. The woman hadn't changed much, he thought: fuller of body, a patch of gray in her hair, but otherwise—He bowed. 'Good day, my lady Alisabeta,' he said.

'Oh!' Her mouth fell open. She swayed on her feet. He was afraid she was about to faint. The irony left him.

'I'm sorry,' he exclaimed. He caught her hands. She leaned on him an instant. 'I'm so sorry. I never meant—I mean—'

She took a long breath and straightened. Her laugh was shaky. 'You surprised me for fair,' she said. 'Come in.'

He followed her. The room beyond was sunny, quiet, book-lined. She offered him a chair. 'W-w-would you like a glass of beer?' She bustled nervously about. 'Or I can make some tea. If you'd rather. That is . . . tea. Coffee?'

'Beer is fine, thanks.' His Maurai was fairly fluent; any scientist had to know that language. 'How've you been?'

'V-very well. And you?'

'All right.'

A stillness grew. He stared at his knees, wishing he hadn't come. She put down two glasses of beer on a table beside him, took a chair opposite, and regarded him for a long while. When finally he looked up, he saw she had drawn on some reserve of steadiness deeper than his own. The color had returned to her face. She even smiled.

'I never expected you would find us, you know,' she said.

'I wasn't sure I would myself,' he mumbled. 'Thought I'd try, though, as long as I was here. No harm in trying,

I thought. Why didn't you change your name or your home base or something?'

'We considered it. But our mission had been so ultrasecret. And Makintairu is a common N'Zealanner name. We didn't plan to do anything but sink back into the obscurity of plain sailor folk. That's all we ever were, you realize.'

'I wasn't sure about that. I thought from the way you handled yourselves—I figured you for special operatives.'

'Oh, heavens, no. Intelligence had decided the truth was less likely to come out if the advance agents were a bona fide merchant crew, that had never been involved in such work before and never would be again. We got some training for the job, but not much, really.'

'I guess the standard of the Sea People is just plain high, then,' Lorn said. 'Must come from generations of taking genetics into consideration when couples want to have kids, eh? That'd never work in my culture, I'm sorry to say. Not the voluntary way you do it, anyhow. We're too damned possessive.'

'But we could never do half the things you've accomplished,' she replied. 'Desert reclamation, for instance. We simply couldn't organize that many people that efficiently for so long a time.'

He drank half his beer and fumbled in a breast pocket for a cigar. 'Can you satisfy my curiosity on one point?' he asked. 'These past years I've wondered and wondered about what happened. I can only figure your bunch must have been in direct contact with each other. Your operation was too well coordinated for anything else. And yet you weren't packing portable radios. Are you telepaths, or what?'

'Goodness, no!' She laughed, more relaxed every minute. 'We did have portable radios. Ultraminiaturized sets, surgically implanted, using body heat for power. Hooked directly into the nervous system, and hence using too broad a band for conventional equipment to read. It was rather like telepathy, I'll admit. I missed the sensation when the sets were removed afterward.'

'Hm.' Somewhat surer of his own self, he lit the cigar and squinted at her through the first smoke. 'You're spilling your secrets mighty freely on such short notice, aren't you?'

'The transceivers aren't a secret any longer. That's more my professional interest than yours, and you've been wrapped up in preparations for your convention, so evidently you haven't heard. But the basic techniques were released last year, as if freshly invented. The psychologists are quite excited about it as a research and therapeutic tool.'

'I see. And as for the fact my lab was not raided by corsairs but by an official Federation party—' Lorn's mouth tightened under the moustache. 'You're confessing that too, huh?'

'What else can I do, now you've found us? Kill you? There was far too much killing.' Her hand stole across the table until it rested on his. The dark eyes softened; he saw a trace of tears. 'Lorn,' she murmured, 'we hated our work.'

'I suppose.' He sat quiet, looked at his cigar end, drew heavily on the smoke, and looked back at her. 'I was nearly as bitter as Dhananda at first . . . bitter as the whole Brahmard caste. The biggest accomplishment of my life, gone. Not even enough notes left to reconstruct the plans. No copies had been sent to the mainland, you see, for security reasons. We were afraid of spies; or someone might've betrayed us out of sheer hysteria, associating nuclear energy with the Judgment. Though, supposing we had saved the blueprints, there'd have been no possibility of rebuilding. Beneghal's treasury was exhausted. People were starving, close to revolt in some districts, this had been so expensive, and nothing ever announced to show for their taxes. Did you stop to think of that? That you were robbing Beneghali peasants who never did you any harm?'

'Often,' she said. 'But remember, the tax collectors had skinned them first. The cost of that reactor project would have bought them a great deal of happiness and advancement. As witness the past several years, after the

168

Brahmards buckled down to attaining more modest goals.'

'But the reactor was working! Unlimited energy. In ten years' time, Beneghal could've been overflowing with every industrial material. The project would have paid off a thousand times over. And you smashed it!'

Lorn sank back in his chair. Slowly, his fist unclenched. 'We couldn't prove the job had not been done by pirates,' he said without tone. 'Certainly Beneghal couldn't declare war on the mighty Maurai Federation without proof enough to bring in a lot of indignant allies. Especially when your government offered such a whopping big help to relieve the famine. . . . But we could suspect. We could feel morally certain. And angry. God, how angry!

'Until—' He sighed. 'I don't know. When I came home and got back into the swing of my regular work . . . and bit by bit re-realized what a decent, helpful, ungreedy bunch your people always have been . . . I finally decided you must've had some reason that seemed good to you. I couldn't imagine what, but . . . oh, I don't know. Reckon we have to take some things on faith, or life would get too empty. Don't worry, Alisabeta. I'm not going to make any big public revelation. Wouldn't do any good, anyway. Too much water's gone under that particular dam. Your government might be embarrassed, but no one would care enough to make real trouble. Probably most folks would think I was lying. So I'll keep my mouth shut.' He raised blue eyes that looked like a child's, a child who has been struck without knowing what the offense was. 'But could you tell me why? What you were scared of?'

'Surely,' said Alisabeta. She leaned farther across the table, smiled with great gentleness, and stroked his cheek, just once. 'Poor well-meaning man!

'There's no secret about our motives. The only secret is that we did take action. Our arguments have been known for decades—ever since the theoretical possibility of controlled hydrogen fusion began to be seriously discussed. That's why the Brahmards were so furtive about their project. They knew we'd put pressure on to stop them.'

'Yes, Dhananda always said you were jealous. Afraid you'd lose your position as the world's top power.'

'Well, frankly, that's part of it. By and large, we like the way things are going. We want to stay able to protect what we like. We weren't afraid Beneghal would embark on a career of world conquest or any such stupidity. But given atomic energy, they could manufacture such quantities of war matériel as to be invincible—explosives, motor vehicles, jet planes, yes, nuclear weapons. Once they presented us with a *fait accompli* like that, we wouldn't be able to do anything about events. Beneghal would take the lead. Our protests could be ignored; eventually, no one anywhere would listen to us. We could only regain leadership by embarking on a similar program. And the War of Judgment proved where a race like that would end!'

'M-m-m . . . yes—'

'Even if we refrained from trying for a nuclear capability, others would not. You understand that's why the Brahmards never have told the world what they were doing. They see as well as us the scramble to duplicate their feat that would immediately follow.

'But there's a subtle and important reason why Beneghal in particular shouldn't be allowed to dominate the scene. The Brahmards are missionaries at heart. They think the entire planet should be converted to their urban-industrial ideal. Whereas we believe—and we have a good deal of psychodynamic science to back us—we believe the many different cultures that grew up in isolation during the dark ages should continue their own evolution. Think, Lorn. The most brilliant eras of history were always when alien societies came into reasonably friendly contact. When Egypt and Crete met in the Eighteenth Dynasty; Phoenician, Persian, Greek in classical times; Nippon and Sina in the Nara period; Byzantium, Asia, and Europe crossbreeding to make the Renaissance—and, yes, our era right now!

'Oh, surely, the Brahmard approach has much to offer.

We don't want to suppress it. Neither do we want it to take over the world. But given the power and productivity, the speed and volume of traffic, the resource consumption, the population explosion . . . given everything that your project would have brought about . . . the machine culture *would* absorb the whole human race again. As it did before the Judgment. Not by conquest, but by being so much stronger materially that everyone would have to imitate it or go under.'

Breathless, Alisabeta reached for her glass. Lorn rubbed his chin. 'M-m-m . . . maybe,' he said. 'If industrialism can feed and clothe people better, though, doesn't it deserve to win out?'

'Who says it can?' she argued. 'It can feed and clothe more people, yes. But not necessarily better. And are sheer numbers any measure of quality, Lorn? Don't you want to leave some places on Earth where a man can go to be alone?

'And, too, suppose industrialism did begin to spread. Think of the transition period. I told you once about the horrors that are a matter of historical record, when the ancient Communists set out to westernize their countries overnight. That would happen again. Not that the Brahmards would do it; they're good men. But other leaders elsewhere—half barbarian, childishly eager for power and prestige, breaking their home cultures to bits in their impatience—such leaders would arise.

'Of course it's wrong that people go poor and hungry. But that problem has more than one solution. Each civilization can work out its own. We do it in the Islands by exploiting the seas and limiting our population. You do it in Merica by dry farming and continental trade. The Okkaidans do it by making moderation into a way of life. The Sberyaks are developing a fascinating system of reindeer ranches. And on and on. How much we learn from each other!'

'Even from Beneghal,' Lorn said dryly.

'Yes,' she nodded, quite grave. 'Machine techniques especially. Although . . . well, let them do as they please, but no one in the Islands envies them. I really don't

171

think their way—the old way—is anything like the best. Man isn't made for it. If industrialism was so satisfying, why did the industrial world commit suicide?'

'I suppose that's another reason you're afraid of atomic energy,' he said. 'Atomic war.'

She shook her head. 'We aren't afraid. We could develop the technology ourselves and keep anyone else from doing so. But we don't want that tight a control on the world. We think Maurai interference should be kept to an absolute minimum.'

'Nevertheless,' he said, sharp-toned, 'you do interfere.'

'True,' she agreed. 'That's another lesson we've gotten from history. The ancients could have saved themselves if they'd had the courage—been hardhearted enough—to act before things snowballed. If the democracies had suppressed every aggressive dictatorship in its infancy; or if they had simply enforced their ideal of an armed world government at the time when they had the strength to do— Well.' She glanced down. Her hand left his and went slowly across her abdomen; a redness crept into her cheeks. 'No,' she said, 'I'm sorry people got hurt, that day at Annaman, but I'm not sorry about the end result. I always planned to have children, you see.'

Lorn stirred. His cigar had gone out. He relit it. The first puff was as acrid as expected. Sunlight slanted in the windows to glow on the wooden floor, on a batik rug from Smatra and a statuette of strangely disturbing beauty from somewhere in Africa.

'Well,' he said, 'I told you I've dropped my grudge. I guess you don't figure to hold atomic energy down forever.'

'Oh no. Someday, in spite of everything we do, Earth will have grown unified and dull. Then it will again be time to try for the stars.'

'So I've heard various of your thinkers claim. Me, though . . . philosophically, I don't like your attitude. I'm resigned to it, sure. Can't have every wish granted in this life. I did get the fun of working on that project, at least. But damn it, Alisabeta, I think you're wrong. If your society can't handle something big and new like the

172

tamed atom, why, by Oktai, you've proved your society isn't worth preserving.'

He felt instantly regretful and started to apologize: no offense meant, just a difference of viewpoint and— But she didn't give him a chance to say the words. She raised her head, met his gaze, and smiled like a cat.

'Our society can't handle something new?' she murmured. 'Oh, my dear Lorn, what do you think we were doing that day?'

THE END

EARTH ABIDES *by* GEORGE R. STEWART

Earth Abides is one of the few SF novels to break the barriers of SF readership and reach a huge and universal audience. Winner of the International Fantasy Award and First Choice of the Science Fiction Book Club, it tells of the death of civilisation and of the brave new race that emerges—stronger, self-reliant, primitive . . .
It is the story of Isherwood Williams and a small handful like him, who rise from the ashes of a destroyed world and begin again . . .

0 552 11194 5 — £1.00

A CANTICLE FOR LEIBOWITZ
   by WALTER M. MILLER, Jr.

A Canticle For Leibowitz is one of the great legendary novels of SF. It begins twelve hundred years after the Fallout. The darkest of dark ages has passed and human intelligence has been reborn. And in a monastery cell the monks and novices of the Blessed Order of Leibowitz pore over the records left by the Saint—then, fearfully, tentatively, they begin to experiment with electric light . . .

0 552 11178 3 — £1.25

DRAGONSONG *by* ANNE McCAFFREY

Menolly-Mistress of Music, Ward of Fire Lizards

Every two hundred years or so, shimmering threads fall, raining black ruin on Pern. The great dragons of Pern hurl themselves through the beleaguered skies, flaming tongues of fire to destroy deadly Thread and save the Planet. It was not Treadfall that made Menolly unhappy. It was her father who betrayed her ambition to be a Harper, who thwarted their love of music. Menolly had no choice but to run away. She came upon a group of fire lizards, wild relatives of the fire-breathing dragons. Her music swirled about them; she taught nine to sing. . . . Suddenly Menolly was no longer alone.

0 552 10661 5 — £1.25

DRAGONSINGER *by* ANNE McCAFFREY

When Menolly, daughter of Yanas Sea Holder, arrived at the Harper Craft Hall, she came in style, aboard a bronze dragon followed by her nine fire lizards. The Masterharper of Pern aware of her unique skills, had chosen her as his only girl apprentice. But the holdness girl had first to overcome many heartaches in this strange new life. Two things sustained her; her devoted lizards—a subject on which she was fitted to instruct her Masters—and the music . . . music of transcendent beauty, music-making where at last she was accepted. In the great Hall, Menolly could fulfill her destiny.

0 552 10881 2 — £1.50

A SELECTED LIST OF
SCIENCE FICTION AND FANTASY
in CORGI

THE PRICES SHOWN BELOW WERE CORRECT AT THE TIME OF GOING TO PRESS (JUNE '81).

All these books are available at your bookshop or newsagent, or can be ordered direct from the publisher. Just tick the titles you want and fill in the form below.

NAME (block letters) ....

ADDRESS ....

(JUNE '81) ....